THE INTERVAL

THE INTERVAL

A NOVEL

NEIL POWELL

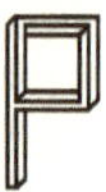

Published by
The Studio Of Neil Powell

ISDN: 979-8-9944172-3-2
Type: Baskerville, IBM Plex Sans
Cover design: Neil Powell
© 2026 The Studio Of NeilPowell

Dedicated to my Mother,
Thanks for all the encouragement.

Table Of Contents

CHAPTER ONE

EMERGENCE

Day 1

The first disk rose out of the Pacific before dawn, though no one agreed on the moment until much later.

Deep-ocean pressure sensors registered the disturbance first. A vertical displacement without seismic accompaniment, logged automatically and flagged for review by systems that did not yet know what they were looking at. There was no shock wave, no rupture, no sound. Just a sudden change in resistance, as if something enormous had decided to move and the water had decided to let it.

On a monitoring vessel several hundred miles away, a technician leaned closer to his screen, certain the numbers were wrong. He re-calibrated, then re-calibrated again. The readouts stabilized. The disturbance was still there.

Minutes later, the surface began to change.

It did not break. It did not boil or churn. The ocean did not part so much as yield, folding away from a rising absence of light. At first it looked like shadow lifting through darker shadow, an interruption where reflection should have been. Then the curve resolved—smooth, matte, continuous— emerging edge-first from the water.

No wave followed.

That detail unsettled the crew watching from a nearby Coast Guard cutter more than the size did. Tons of seawater should have been displaced violently. Instead, the surface slid away from the object and closed behind it, leaving only a faint disturbance that faded almost immediately.

The edge rose higher.

It was flat and wide, nearly a mile across, rotating with deliberate slowness. The disk itself extended beyond the frame of every camera pointed at it, its curvature suggesting a diameter that dwarfed cities without offering a single complete view.

It stood upright, as if gravity had been reassigned.

Then it began to roll.

Not propelled, not accelerated. Simply rotating, the edge touching the surface of the sea at a single, precise line. Where contact occurred, the water did not compress or spray. It changed.

Sensors anchored to the seabed went silent as the disk passed over them. Not crushed. Not severed. Simply ended. The data stream stopped mid-transmission, as though the instruments had never existed.

Behind the contact point, the water looked different. Clearer. Colder. Structured in ways the software could not immediately describe.

Within minutes, similar reports arrived.

A second disk surfaced in the Indian Ocean.

Another in the South Atlantic.

Two more rose through Arctic ice without cracking it.

By sunrise, there were dozens.

By midmorning, hundreds.

They did not surface randomly.

Each disk followed its own path, curving gently across the planet's surface, rolling out of the oceans and onto land without hesitation. Satellite models attempted to plot their trajectories and failed. Every simulation that predicted overlap or collision produced errors. The paths behaved like solved problems no one had been given the equations for.

Mountains did not slow them.

When one disk reached the coast of South America, it touched land and continued forward. The edge met sand, rock, concrete, and steel without registering resistance. The city in its path did not collapse. Buildings did not shatter or buckle. They were simply gone after the disk passed, replaced by land that looked older than memory and newer than construction.

A corridor, nearly a mile wide, cut cleanly through everything it encountered.

Downtown districts.

Rail hubs.

Power stations.

There was no trench. No groove. No scar.

From a distance, it looked as though nothing had happened at all—until you tried to cross from one side to the other and realized the world no longer connected the way it used to.

People could walk away from the disks.

That was the first comfort the world clung to.

They moved slowly enough that evacuation was possible. Slow enough to pack a car. Slow enough to stand on a hillside and watch one approach for hours. Slow enough that panic struggled to take hold.

But they did not stop.

Markets reacted before governments did.

Insurance exchanges froze as actuarial models failed simultaneously. Shipping routes were severed mid-voyage. Ports closed not because they were destroyed, but because their logic had been interrupted. No one knew how to insure a future where the ground itself could be reorganized without damage.

Governments issued statements urging calm. The word, "advisory," appeared and spread, soft and noncommittal. There was no declaration of emergency, no call to arms. There was nothing to fight.

Religious leaders spoke within hours.

Some called the disks judgment. Others called them mercy. A few said nothing at all, waiting to see which interpretation would survive the first week.

Online, names multiplied. Wheels. Harvesters. Returning Measures. A preacher in Louisiana referred to them as reclamation made visible, and the phrase spread faster than any official designation ever could have.

By the time the term, "Reclaimer," appeared in a classified briefing, it was already too late to control the language.

On a bluff overlooking what had once been a coastal highway, a woman stood with her phone in her hand and watched a disk approach.

It was taller than mountains. Wider than cities. Upright,

silent, and patient.

Behind her, the ocean sounded the same as it always had. Birds called inland, confused but alive. Nothing about the moment felt urgent, and that terrified her more than any siren could have.

The disk continued its slow, indifferent roll toward the land.

And across the world, people realized the same thing at roughly the same time:

This was not an invasion.

It was not a warning.

It was not something that could be negotiated with, out-run, or meaningfully opposed.

It was a process.

And it had already begun.

CHAPTER TWO

ALIGNMENT

Day 2

By the second day, the problem was no longer discovery. It was coordination.

Maps were redrawn constantly. Not because the objects changed course—they did not—but because the assumptions embedded in the maps no longer held. Borders assumed permanence. Roads assumed continuity. Jurisdictions assumed edges that stayed where they were put. None of that survived contact with a mile-wide line that advanced steadily and ignored what it crossed.

Briefings opened with projections. They always did. Clean paths traced across terrain, each annotated with time estimates that felt precise until they weren't. The language was careful, provisional. Updates would follow. Adjustments would be made. There was time, as long as time behaved.

The shadow complicated everything.

In regions far ahead of any object's projected path, daylight began to thin without explanation. Morning light dimmed and returned. Noon slipped briefly into dusk and corrected itself. Weather reports remained accurate. Astronomical models held. Only the ground noticed the discrepancy.

Meetings were rescheduled around light windows. Press briefings paused until brightness returned. Schools shortened days that had already begun. In some cities, streetlights came on at lunchtime and stayed on through the afternoon—not because visibility required it, but because people needed confirmation that systems still responded.

On internal displays, the term "rolling object," began to appear. It was chosen for its neutrality rather than its usefulness. The abbreviation RO followed shortly after, not as a classification, but as a way to save space on crowded screens.

The objects were spaced deliberately.

Far enough apart to avoid overlap.

Close enough to ensure coverage.

No region could claim exemption. No border offered protection. Every model that relied on redirection, deflection, or obstruction failed quietly, producing outputs that looked complete until someone asked what they were supposed to change.

Someone suggested staggered evacuations.

Someone else asked where people were meant to go when corridors were continuous.

The answer arrived too slowly to matter.

Within forty-eight hours, a controlled engagement was authorized.

The language avoided the word attack. Officials referred to it instead as a characterization exercise—an effort to determine response thresholds, material limits, and potential deterrence.

The selected object was rolling through uninhabited desert. Airspace was cleared. Observation assets were positioned well beyond any projected interaction zone.

The first strike was kinetic. The round impacted precisely where predicted.

Nothing happened.

No deflection. No visible damage. No audible response. Sensors recorded the impact as a momentary absence—data terminating at the contact point and resuming immediately behind it.

Subsequent deployments followed in rapid succession. High-explosive. Armor-piercing. Directed energy. Each executed cleanly. Each producing the same result.

The object did not slow.

It did not accelerate.

It did not respond.

After-action reports were filed with language that grew increasingly careful. Phrases like weapon ineffectiveness and non-interaction outcome appeared and were left undefined.

By the end of the day, escalation options were exhausted—not by resistance, but by irrelevance.

In one coastal state, evacuation orders were issued, revised, and reissued within a single afternoon as projections tightened. Traffic moved, then stalled. Drivers turned back when the shadow passed overhead, convinced the worst had been delayed. By the time the light returned, the edge was already closer than expected.

No one was trapped.

No one was harmed.

No one could say exactly when they had waited too long.

The clocks remained correct.

That was part of the problem.

The sun rose when it should have. Forecasts matched the sky. Astronomical explanations held. Only the surface of the world behaved as if something were wrong, dimming under a shadow that did not belong to any cloud system or celestial event.

Air traffic controllers learned to read the situation indirectly. Radar behaved normally. Transponders responded. What changed was the light beyond the glass, thinning across runways and terminals in slow, deliberate bands. Flights were delayed not because conditions were unsafe, but because passengers could not reconcile the hour with what they saw outside.

The urgency never announced itself.

There were no sirens.

No countdowns.

No single moment that demanded escalation.

Instead, there was accumulation.

Clearances arrived after relevance.

Decisions were approved for places that no longer connected the way they had that morning.

Plans were correct on paper and obsolete by the time they circulated.

From orbit, the planet looked threaded.

Thousands of narrow, moving lines crossed oceans and continents alike, each one tall enough to pierce cloud layers, each one balanced on an edge wide enough to register only where it touched. Their shadows intersected briefly, then separated again, creating regions where daylight came and went twice in the same afternoon.

Analysts tried to model the shadow first. It seemed easier than modeling the objects themselves. The equations worked briefly, then failed as angles shifted. The shadow refused to behave like a consequence. It acted more like an accompanying feature.

In public statements, officials avoided the word darkness. They spoke instead of temporary dimming and variable light conditions. The phrases circulated briefly and then fell away, replaced by silence when no better language followed.

By the end of the second day, something subtle had changed.

The objects were no longer discussed as arrivals.

They were discussed as paths.

What mattered was not where they came from, but where they would be when decisions caught up. And even that question began to feel theoretical as the gap between observation and action narrowed without ever closing.

The light would thin.

The edge would advance.

And whatever time there had been would continue to be spent elsewhere.

CHAPTER THREE

THRESHOLD

Day 3

By the third day, the objects were no longer being watched.

They were being accommodated.

The rolling continued at the same measured pace. Five miles per hour became a background number, absorbed into forecasts and footnotes. People learned to say it without emphasis, the way they spoke about tides or wind speed. Slow enough to feel manageable. Fast enough to punish delay.

The shadow refused to settle.

In some regions it arrived at nearly the same hour each day, early enough to anticipate but late enough to disrupt. In others, it slipped forward or backward without pattern, dimming the world briefly and then releasing it. The light never left completely. It thinned, faded, behaved as if it were negotiating.

People began to plan around it.

Office hours shifted by half-days. Morning meetings were rescheduled to full-light windows. Schools experimented with staggered schedules, then abandoned them when parents complained that nothing lined up. Transit systems issued advisories that meant nothing to commuters who could see perfectly well and still felt wrong stepping outside.

The clocks remained correct.

That was part of the problem.

The sun rose when it should have. Forecasts matched the sky. Astronomical explanations held. Only the ground noticed the discrepancy, darkening under a shadow that did not belong to any cloud system or celestial event.

Maps were still being updated, but they were consulted less often. Routes changed faster than guidance could circulate. At some point, the maps stopped being used for movement and were referenced only to confirm what had already happened.

People stopped looking at the objects directly.

At first this was practical. The scale resisted observation. There was nowhere for the eye to rest. Looking up caused strain—neck pain, headaches, a sense of vertigo that passed only when attention shifted elsewhere. But over time, the avoidance became habitual. You didn't need to see the object to know it was there. The shadow was enough. The corridor it left behind was undeniable.

In one suburb, residents gathered to discuss repainting crosswalks that now ended in open ground. The motion passed narrowly. The repainting was scheduled for the following week. By the time the crew arrived, the street itself had shifted from relevance.

No one was injured.

That fact continued to complicate response.

Emergency rooms reported no surge. Hospitals remained within capacity. The absence of casualties resisted every attempt to escalate language. The objects did not pursue. They did not accelerate. They did not react to proximity. They edited.

Insurance systems strained under precision rather than destruction. Claims were accepted, paused, revised, and accepted again under evolving definitions of loss. Adjusters photographed properties that no longer aligned with their addresses. Files were opened for places that could not be revisited.

The shadow reached places before the news did.

In agricultural regions, it cut across fields during what should have been peak daylight. Sensors registered drops in photosynthesis that did not align with weather patterns. The data was flagged, then flagged again. Farmers adjusted schedules, then adjusted them back. The light kept leaving and returning at the wrong hours, long enough to matter, short enough to be ignored.

Children adapted faster than adults.

They learned which playgrounds would darken without warning. They adjusted games to account for sudden shade. In classrooms, drawings began to shift. The sun was still present, but it was no longer centered. Sometimes it appeared twice. Sometimes not at all. Teachers corrected this gently, then stopped correcting it.

From orbit, the planet looked annotated.

Long, narrow bands crossed continents and oceans alike, their shadows intersecting briefly before separating again. Analysts counted intersections, then stopped. The number did not change anything.

The urgency never announced itself.
There was no siren moment.
No single threshold crossed.
No sentence that ended in now.
Instead, there was erosion.
A delay here.
A missed window there.
A plan approved after the reason for it had passed.

By the end of the third day, a phrase began circulating quietly in internal communications, then publicly, then everywhere: Manageable Condition.

It was meant to reassure.

What it actually meant was that people had begun to accept that the time they were losing would not be returned.

The light would come back.

The edge would move on.

And whatever had been possible yesterday would remain just barely out of reach tomorrow.

CHAPTER FOUR

PROXIMITY

Day 3

The military reached the object outside Fort Devens before the crowds did.

That was not an accident.

The perimeter went up in the early hours of the morning, floodlights stabbing into mist, temporary barriers unfolding with the practiced speed of people who had rehearsed for emergencies that never looked like this. Soldiers moved quietly, efficiently, without the shouted urgency of drills. Orders passed hand-to-hand, not over loudspeakers. No one wanted this to feel like a spectacle.

The object did not acknowledge the perimeter.

Up close, the edge carried no sense of proportion. It rose beyond the mist, beyond the reach of floodlights, beyond anything the base could meaningfully frame. Twenty-five miles of height expressed itself not as distance, but as absence of an end.

It rolled forward at the same pace it had maintained since emerging from the Atlantic, its immense, upright edge cutting across scrub land and abandoned access roads without deviation. The contact line where it touched the ground remained impossibly clean, a seam rather than a wound.

The line advanced continuously, not sliding, not scraping, but rotating—each section of the edge touching the earth once and never again.

A convoy of armored vehicles idled at a safe distance, engines low, exhaust hanging in the air. Engineers in protective gear approached on foot, carrying equipment that looked inadequate even before it failed.

They stopped fifty yards from the edge.

The light thinned briefly while they waited. Floodlights compensated automatically, then shut off again when the brightness returned. No one looked up. The timing was logged.

The first drone went up without ceremony. It rose smoothly, stabilized, and drifted toward the disk's surface, its camera feed relayed to half a dozen monitors inside the mobile command unit.

The image was unsatisfying.

There was no distortion. No glare. No visible resistance. The drone's instruments returned stable readings until, without warning, the feed cut to gray and the drone ceased to exist—not destroyed, not deflected, simply absent beyond a boundary no one could see.

No one ordered a second launch.

What proximity meant began to change.

By late morning, reports arrived from elsewhere—far from Fort Devens, far from any declared perimeter.

The reports did not describe the same object. They described the same behavior, repeated hundreds of times, separated by geography but identical in effect.

A major bridge several states away had begun to behave incorrectly.

Not dangerously. Incorrectly.

The first complaint came from a cyclist who said the roadway felt wrong near the eastern span, as if the surface were breathing. Maintenance crews inspected the expansion joints and found nothing outside specification. Metal expanded. Everyone agreed.

On the second day, sensors registered a variance small enough to be logged automatically and ignored. The bridge had been designed to move. Movement was proof of intelligence.

By the third day, drivers corrected for a curve that did not exist on any plan. The roadway dipped—not enough to alarm, just enough to require attention. A delivery truck scraped a guardrail at low speed. The driver blamed the wind.

Engineers convened beneath the deck. Someone mentioned tides. Someone else said thermal stress. No one used the other word. Invasion.

The bridge remained open.
The closure order cleared review three hours later.

On the fourth morning, traffic slowed without instruction. Cars eased forward into fog. From inside the vehicles, nothing appeared wrong.

The fog arrived early that day, coinciding with a dimming that had already been reported in three other regions and dismissed as unrelated.

The first car stopped because there was nowhere else to

go.

The road ended cleanly. Not torn. Not broken. Just absent. Paint lines reached forward and stopped.

Engines idled. Radios played. A driver stepped out, hands on hips, waiting for the rest of the bridge to arrive.

Maps adapted quickly. Routes recalculated. The bridge remained visible on every interface, still labeled, still offering directions no one could complete.

By nightfall, the lights stayed on. From shore, it looked unchanged—elegant, complete, reaching confidently into dark air.

It was listed as inactive.

Back at Fort Devens, the perimeter was pushed another hundred yards out.

The adjustment was entered as a precaution. No one believed it would be the last.

No announcement was made. Stakes were driven in. Barriers repositioned. The new distance felt safer without being safer in any measurable way.

Proximity, it turned out, was not about how close you could get.

It was about how far away you decided to stand.

CHAPTER FIVE

EXPOSURE

Day 3-6

In northern Spain, a line of hikers formed along a rural ridge outside León, pacing the slow advance of a rolling object across scrub land and stone terraces. Some carried folding chairs. Some brought thermoses. They took turns walking close to the boundary, stopping every few minutes to look back and confirm the edge had moved at all. Children treated it like a strange parade float that never arrived.

Someone began keeping time out loud.

"One meter," a woman announced after nearly an hour, her voice amused and disbelieving.

Applause rippled briefly and then faded into embarrassed laughter.

The object rose beside them like a wall that refused metaphor. Upright, matte, and silent, it extended upward beyond weather, beyond aircraft, beyond the range where the eye could hold continuity. At approximately twenty-five miles tall, it did not present itself as an object so much as a vertical condition.

Its width was the thing people could grasp once they

understood it: nearly a mile of uninterrupted edge, rolling forward without sway or deviation. It did not loom in the way buildings did. It erased lateral context instead, like a fact too broad to step around.

They posted photos. The photos went everywhere.

In western Australia, a mining town shut down its operations and dragged picnic tables into the path of an approaching object, setting them carefully just outside the projected boundary. Someone brought a sound system. Someone else brought beer. The gathering acquired a name before it acquired a reason.

A Passing Party.

No one organized it formally. People simply arrived. They grilled food. They told stories. They waited.

When the object finally reached the clearing near sunset, the music stopped on its own. Conversations softened. Phones came out.

Someone laughed and said it sounded like the thing itself ought to have a name.

Passer, another voice offered, without emphasis.

The word stayed.

No one announced it. No one explained it. It moved the way the object did—slowly, without insistence, and then all at once it was everywhere.

No one tried to capture the whole of it. There was no angle wide enough. The Passer continued forward, indifferent, its edge passing with a precision that made fences, plans, and jokes feel provisional.

By the end of the week, similar scenes were unfolding elsewhere.

Not protests.

Not celebrations.

Just people standing near something vast enough to make reaction feel optional.

In the Midwest, families parked along service roads and watched the shadow slide across fields before the edge arrived. Children ran ahead to see how far the light would thin, then ran back, laughing when it returned. Parents checked watches, then checked nothing at all. The timing was shared in group chats as if it were weather.

In South America, a bus company began advertising "edge rides"—routes that paralleled projected paths long enough for passengers to feel included without being delayed. The service sold out immediately. Reviews mentioned comfort, predictability, and the strange relief of having nothing to do but keep pace.

Online, the tone shifted.

Early posts had been crowded with measurements and disbelief. Those gave way to comparison photos, then to routine updates: today's pace, today's light, today's place where the world briefly did not connect. The language softened. The Passer was no longer always approaching. Often, it was simply there.

Officials discouraged gathering near the corridors. Advisories were issued. They were ignored politely. The Passers did not reward attention, and they did not punish it. People learned the distance that felt respectful and stayed there.

The shadow helped.

It arrived first, thinning the day without drama, giving people time to set down what they were doing and look up. When the light returned, the edge was closer than expected.

When it passed, the ground felt unchanged enough to invite conversation.

No one could agree on what accompaniment meant.

Some said it was witness.

Others called it defiance.

A few insisted it was boredom finally finding a scale large enough to occupy it.

Psychologists were interviewed. Anthropologists were consulted. The conclusions did not travel far.

What did travel were the videos: long, quiet clips where nothing happened except movement too slow to trust. Viewers watched them for minutes at a time, then longer, waiting for proof. The proof never came. The Passers kept moving.

Five miles per hour was slow enough to invite company. Fast enough to make leaving feel like a choice you might regret later.

By the time accompaniment became common, the urgency had already changed shape. It no longer pressed from ahead. It accumulated alongside, minute by minute, step for step, like a companion that did not speak.

And in that shared pace, something subtle occurred.

People began to feel that if they stayed close enough, long enough, the meaning might arrive with the object.

It did not.

The edge passed.

The light returned.

And the world continued, edited but intact, leaving behind only the sense that whatever had once required reaction no longer asked for it.

CHAPTER SIX

ADAPTATION

Day 7

By the end of the first week, the maps stopped pretending they were temporary.

What had begun as projected paths—dotted lines, shaded bands, polite overlays meant to reassure—hardened into something closer to infrastructure. The corridors carved by the Passers were now fixed features, mile-wide absences that did not collapse or erode, did not invite rebuilding, did not behave like disaster zones so much as new geography.

The soil did not resist rebuilding. It simply failed to cooperate with it.

Stakes driven into the ground loosened overnight. Survey markers reappeared inches from where they had been placed. Concrete cured unevenly, as if unsure what shape it was meant to remember. Nothing collapsed. Nothing was rejected. It just refused to behave as a foundation.

Jurisdiction failed first.

City boundaries meant nothing to a line that cut through neighborhoods without regard for zoning or tax base. Counties lost continuity. States inherited shapes no one had language for. In one case, a municipal border now existed on opposite sides of a corridor that could not be crossed without hours of detour.

Lawyers tried to keep up.

They failed quietly.

Emergency powers were invoked, revised, invoked again. The word temporary appeared so often in briefings that it began to sound superstitious. No one wanted to be the first to admit that nothing about this felt provisional.

Inside the Federal Emergency Coordination Center, the screens multiplied.

Live feeds. Corridor projections. Evacuation compliance rates. Social sentiment analysis scrolling past in colors no one fully trusted. The room hummed with constant motion, but very little progress.

General Marcus Redding stood near the back, watching.

He had built his career on containment—threats that could be bounded, delayed, or redirected. He was not given to spectacle, and he did not confuse activity with control. What he watched for now was not escalation, but the point at which response stopped mattering.

He had learned long ago that authority revealed itself most clearly at its limits. This—this slow, patient reorganization of the planet—was not a crisis that could be outpaced by procedure. Every response arrived after the fact, trailing behind a process that did not acknowledge response as a variable.

A junior analyst approached him with a tablet, eyes rimmed red from lack of sleep.

"Sir, we're seeing secondary movement."

Redding took the tablet. "Define secondary."

"People," the analyst said. "Not evacuating. Not interfering. Just… following. Along the edges. Some for days."

Redding scrolled. The footage showed long lines of figures moving parallel to the corridors—on foot, on bicycles, in cars that idled when the road ended and resumed when it began again. People camped just outside the boundary, cooking, sleeping, waking to check whether the line had advanced at all.

"They're treating it like some kind of… pilgrimage," the analyst said, uncomfortable with the word.

Redding handed the tablet back. "They're treating it like certainty."

Across the room, a heated discussion rose and fell.

"We can't let this normalize," someone said.

"It already has," someone else replied.

"We need visible control."

"There is no visible control."

That was the problem.

Nothing about the Passers responded to escalation. There was no deterrent posture to adopt, no show of force that altered pace or path. Redding had authorized every tool the doctrine allowed—kinetic, explosive, directed—and watched each one pass through the problem without registering. Even the military's presence now felt ceremonial, uniforms framing an event that refused to acknowledge them.

Redding cleared his throat. The room quieted.

"We are not dealing with an adversary," he said. "We are dealing with a condition."

That word—condition—landed heavily.

Conditions are managed, not defeated.

A regional director spoke up. "We need to decide what to tell people who won't leave."

Redding nodded. "We tell them the truth."

A few heads turned.

"That we don't know what prolonged proximity does," he continued. "That the soil is altered in ways we're still studying. That choosing to stay is a choice, not an act of defiance."

"And if they stay anyway?"

"Then we document," Redding said. "We do not criminalize behavior we can't define as harmful."

Silence followed—not agreement, but recognition.

Elsewhere, the first attempts at infrastructure adaptation began.

Temporary bridges arced over corridors at enormous cost, their construction watched closely for any sign of resistance from the altered ground. There was none. The soil accepted pylons without protest, compacted cleanly, held weight.

People crossed.

People crossed again.

Some cried on the other side.

Others turned back and crossed a second time, as if to prove to themselves that continuity could be rehearsed.

In one city, a mayor proposed rerouting public transit permanently around a corridor that now bisected downtown. The proposal passed unanimously. No one wanted to be remembered as having insisted on restoration.

At the edge of a corridor in Ohio, a man stood holding a cardboard sign that read:

THIS IS THE LINE

No one knew what he meant.

By nightfall, Redding sat alone in his office, lights dimmed, reviewing a briefing he had not yet allowed to circulate. It contained Dr. Elise Halvorsen's preliminary findings, flagged and annotated but not diluted.

He read the phrase again:

Restoration to a prior operational baseline.

Operational.

As if the planet were a system that could be paused and resumed.

Redding closed the file and leaned back, staring at the ceiling.

He had spent his career believing that stability was something governments produced.

Now he understood, with an uncomfortable clarity, that stability was something larger systems allowed—until they didn't.

Outside, the Passers continued their steady movement, one mile of edge at a time.

And everywhere, lines were being redrawn—not just on maps, but in the quiet, unspoken calculations people made about where they stood, what they obeyed, and how much of the world they were willing to let go of.

CHAPTER SEVEN

SIGNALS

Day 7

Lena Ortiz had learned to sleep in pieces.

That habit came from years before the corridors—before the Passers—when disaster zones still behaved like emergencies instead of conditions. Floods. Wildfires. Chemical spills. Places where people arrived assuming they would leave soon.

Lena had been good at those places.

Not at fixing them. At staying long enough to keep things from unraveling further. She understood transition points— how panic crept in when no one was clearly in charge yet, how order could be improvised before authority arrived.

She never stayed because she believed things would return to normal.

She stayed because someone always had to be present when normal failed.

Four hours here. Ninety minutes there. A shallow doze in the passenger seat while someone else took the wheel. The body adjusted when it had to. What didn't adjust was the sense that time itself had loosened—stretched thin by the knowledge that nothing urgent was happening, and that everything was.

She woke to the sound of boots on gravel.

The Passer stood fifty yards away, upright and patient, its immense edge occupying the horizon like a thought no one could finish. Morning light flattened against its matte surface and disappeared. No glare. No reflection. Just absence.

Lena pushed herself upright and stretched, joints protesting. Around her, the temporary observation camp was coming back to life: tents unzipping, radios crackling, someone swearing quietly as they spilled coffee onto the dirt.

"Any change?" she asked, walking toward the perimeter line.

"Same pace," a technician replied without looking up. "About a meter every fifty minutes."

Lena nodded. She had memorized the numbers by now. Everyone had. The slowness had become its own kind of pressure—a constant reminder that decisions could be postponed, but not avoided.

She approached the boundary with a handheld sensor array, stopping just short of the contact line. The air here felt different—not colder or warmer, exactly, but cleaner, as if particulate matter had been selectively edited out. The readings confirmed it. Lower nitrogen oxides. Reduced sulfur compounds. Microbial aerosols rearranged into distributions she had only ever seen in controlled environments.

"Still nothing anomalous?" she asked.

"Depends what you call anomalous," the technician said. "It's all… too tidy."

That word again.

Lena crouched and pressed a gloved hand into the soil behind the Passer. It yielded easily, dark and fine, smelling faintly mineral, faintly alive. She pinched a small amount between her fingers and watched it fall.

"Life density's increasing," she said quietly. "But not cha-otically."

CHAPTER EIGHT

CONTAINMENT

Day 12

The first directive came down without ceremony.

No escalation.

No weapons.

No contact with the disk itself.

But observation—observation was no longer sufficient.

General Caldwell read the order twice, then folded it neatly and set it aside. He had learned to recognize when language was being used to create distance from responsibility. This was one of those times.

"Limited proximity operation," he said aloud, as if naming it would make it smaller. "Environmental interface only."

Around him, the mobile command unit hummed softly. Screens glowed with live feeds from the corridor edge, biometric readouts from the field team, scrolling sensor data that still refused to misbehave in ways anyone could act on.

"Make it clear," Caldwell continued. "No heroics. No improvisation."

A lieutenant nodded. "Yes, sir."

The team assembled quietly.

Six people. Engineers, biologists, one materials specialist who had stopped pretending he knew what to expect. They wore light protective gear—not because it was proven necessary, but because standing this close to the unknown demanded something that looked like preparation.

They approached on foot.

The Passer stood upright ahead of them, its vast, matte edge cutting across the terrain like a thought that had never been spoken aloud. It was not imposing in the way weapons were imposing. It did not threaten. It simply occupied.

The contact line was immaculate.

Caldwell watched from behind the barrier, hands clasped behind his back. He noted the way the team slowed without being told. Not fear—reverence was closer, though he disliked the word.

"Range?" he asked.

"Thirty yards," came the reply. "And closing."

The disk rolled forward with the same deliberate calm it always had. No vibration. No sound beyond the soft displacement of air.

"Hold," Caldwell said.

The team stopped.

One of the engineers knelt and placed a marker stake just behind the boundary, careful not to let it touch the disk. The soil accepted it easily, compacting around the metal as if it had been waiting.

"Growth rate's accelerating," the biologist said, voice tight with focus. "This isn't opportunistic life. It's organized."

"Organized how?" someone asked.

She shook her head. "That's the problem. It doesn't

match any succession model we have."

A portable scanner hummed as it passed over the disk's surface from a cautious distance. It returned nothing useful. No resonance. No reflection. No signature that suggested layers or internal structure.

It was like pointing an instrument at absence.

"Permission to attempt acoustic mapping," the materials specialist said.

Caldwell hesitated, then nodded. "One pulse. Low amplitude."

The device emitted a soft, directional sound—barely audible to the human ear.

The wave vanished.

Not absorbed.

Not reflected.

Simply gone.

The silence afterward felt deliberate.

One of the soldiers shifted his weight. "Sir," he said quietly, "it feels like it knows we're here."

Caldwell didn't respond immediately. He watched the disk's edge trace its line across the ground, steady and exact.

"No," he said finally. "It feels like it doesn't need to."

The team withdrew as the Passer advanced, retreating step by careful step until they were safely beyond the boundary. No alarms sounded. No systems failed dramatically. Nothing happened that could be labeled an incident.

And yet.

Inside the command unit, a technician stared at her screen, frowning. "Sir," she said, "we've got a discrepancy."

Caldwell turned. "Where?"

"Biological uptick," she said. "The soil sample from forty minutes ago—it's already showing integration. Not colonization. Integration."

"Meaning?"

"Meaning whatever's growing there isn't adapting to the environment," she said. "The environment is adapting to it."

Caldwell felt a chill that had nothing to do with temperature.

Outside, the Passer continued forward, its immense width erasing distance as a concept. The team watched in silence as another stretch of ground resolved itself into something new and disturbingly orderly.

No damage.

No debris.

Just replacement.

That night, Caldwell recorded a private note he did not forward.

We attempted engagement today, he said into the recorder. The system acknowledged nothing. The environment responded immediately. This is not a probe. It is not an experiment.

He paused, searching for language that did not drift into myth.

It is a procedure.

He shut off the recorder and sat back, listening to the low hum of generators and the distant quiet beyond the perimeter.

Somewhere beneath all of it, the Passer rolled on—unaware, uninterested, and impossibly certain.

And for the first time since this had begun, Caldwell understood that whatever decision humanity made next would not be judged by whether it succeeded.

Only by whether it mattered.

CHAPTER NINE

MARGINS

Day 14

The Passer reached the outskirts just after dawn.

From the highway overpass, it appeared almost stationary, its upright edge holding against the low sky like a misplaced boundary. Traffic slowed not from instruction but from instinct. Drivers rolled past at reduced speed, windows down, phones raised and then lowered again when framing failed to explain what the eye insisted was present.

The disk did not dominate the landscape so much as interrupt it.

Buildings remained intact on either side of its path until they weren't. There was no visible compression, no debris field, no collapse. Structures simply ceased where the edge had passed, replaced by dark soil already settling into itself. The transition was so precise it resisted the word destruction.

People gathered along the projected boundary hours in advance.

They brought folding chairs, coffee, cameras. Some arrived with children, pointing toward the approaching edge as if to a distant parade. Others stood farther back, hands in pockets, saying nothing. No one crossed the line before it arrived.

The Passer continued forward.

Its surface absorbed light without reflection, offering no texture to fix on. The eye searched for seams or irregularities and found none. Scale became abstract. The disk was too large to register as an object and too precise to register as landscape.

A man near the front stepped forward, then stopped himself, as if startled by his own movement. He laughed quietly and retreated to the curb.

When the Passer reached the first row of buildings, nothing dramatic occurred. The edge touched brick and glass with the same indifference it had shown the road. There was no sound beyond wind redirected around a shape too large to acknowledge resistance.

Moments later, the buildings were gone.

Not flattened.

Not reduced.

Gone.

Behind the disk, the corridor opened—dark, fine-grained soil stretching the full width of the path, already receptive to thin green growth that traced no familiar pattern.

The growth was not grass, though it borrowed the color. It did not blade or clump or vine. It rose in fine, jointless filaments, evenly spaced, as if placed rather than grown. No root structures broke the surface. No signs of competition appeared. Each strand occupied its space completely, neither crowding nor yielding.

The air changed first.

It carried the faint, unmistakable scent of clean rain—the

kind that fell after heat, after dust, after long dryness. Not the sharpness of ozone, not the sweetness of plants, but something clearer than both. A smell people recognized without being able to name, because it belonged to memory more than chemistry.

It was the smell of weather that had washed a place without leaving damage behind.

The green did not advance. It did not creep outward from the corridor's edge. It existed only where the Passer had been, as if responding to a condition that no longer applied anywhere else.

Someone said, "Do you smell that?"

No one answered.

The Passer moved on.

As it advanced, people adjusted position automatically, stepping back or sideways to maintain distance without instruction. The crowd thinned, then regrouped farther along the path. No one shouted. No one ran.

The absence of urgency unsettled observers more than panic would have.

By late morning, local authorities arrived and established a perimeter that functioned mostly as suggestion. People complied until they didn't. The Passer ignored all of it.

When the disk passed beyond the last visible structure and into open land, the crowd dispersed unevenly. Some lingered at the corridor's edge, staring down its length as if waiting for something else to arrive. Others left abruptly, as though staying any longer would imply agreement.

The transformed ground remained.

Dark.

Quiet.

Already changing.

And somewhere between arrival and departure, it became clear that watching the Passer was not the same as witnessing an event.

It was closer to noticing a condition.

CHAPTER TEN

LINE OF AUTHORITY

Day 16

General Marcus Redding did not like rooms without windows.

They encouraged speculation. They gave imagination time to wander, which was dangerous when decisions needed to arrive intact. Still, the secure briefing room beneath Northern Command had no windows by design, and tonight it felt smaller than usual.

The screen at the far end of the table showed a static image: an overhead satellite capture of a Passer crossing scrub land in Nevada. The disk's edge was visible only as an absence—a perfectly smooth interruption where texture should have been.

Redding stood with his hands braced on the table, jacket unbuttoned, tie loosened. Around him sat officers, analysts, and civilian liaisons who had stopped pretending this was temporary.

"Let's dispense with the euphemisms," he said. "It didn't pass near the test range. It went through it."

No one argued.

An analyst cleared her throat. "The installation was unoccupied, sir. Personnel had been withdrawn per your directive."

"And the equipment?"

"Gone," she said. "Not destroyed. Removed. As if it had never been placed there."

Redding nodded once. That distinction mattered.

He gestured to the screen. "Show the overlay."

The image shifted. A second layer appeared—before-and-after data rendered in muted colors. Where concrete pads and instrumentation arrays had existed, there was now uninterrupted ground. Darker. Denser. Calm.

"No heat signature," the analyst continued. "No residual radiation. No seismic disturbance. The corridor stabilized within minutes."

Redding folded his arms. "And the strike?"

A pause.

"There was no strike," she said. "No deployment. No engagement window."

"Then what are we calling it?"

The analyst hesitated. "A loss of assets, sir."

Redding exhaled through his nose. "Language is doing a lot of work tonight."

A second screen lit up without prompting. This one carried a civilian seal—transportation, not defense. A liaison leaned forward.

"Sir, we're getting parallel reports from municipal systems," he said. "Unrelated to the corridor."

Redding turned. "Define unrelated."

"Subsurface infrastructure," the liaison said. "Transit. Utilities. Drainage."

The feed changed again.

A subway platform appeared, half submerged, in still water. Bright tile beneath the surface, lights reflected perfectly upside down. A train sat motionless at the edge of the frame, doors closed, power on.

"The pumps are operational," the liaison continued. "No breach detected. No structural failure."

"Then why is it flooded?" Redding asked.

"It isn't flooding," the analyst said carefully. "The grade has shifted."

Another image replaced the first: a service corridor.

Concrete ended in a flat plane, smooth enough to catch the light evenly. Conduit pipes stopped mid-run. Wires were exposed in exact cross-sections, copper ends clean and circular, as if cut by machine. A cable tray ended precisely where the wall ended.

"There's no debris," the analyst said. "Nothing collapsed. The system simply… stops."

Redding stared at the screen.

"Is this within the corridor?" he asked.

"No, sir."

"Then why are we seeing the same geometry?"

No one answered immediately.

A third image appeared—an interface screenshot this time. A transit app, stripped of schedules.

SERVICE SUSPENDED DUE

TO GEOGRAPHIC CONDITIONS

"No estimated restoration time," the liaison said. "That language has been cleared by legal."

Redding closed his eyes briefly.

Line of authority had always meant something to him.

A clean hierarchy. Orders passed downward, responsibility passed upward. But this—this was a failure without an opponent.

"Can we secure it?" he asked.

The analyst shook her head. "There's nothing to secure. The systems are intact. They're just… reassigned."

"Reassigned by what?"

She chose her words carefully. "By whatever determines where space is still valid."

Silence settled over the room.

Redding straightened and adjusted his jacket, the gesture automatic, almost ceremonial.

"Put out an advisory," he said. "Coordinate language across agencies. I don't want five explanations for the same condition."

"Yes, sir."

"And make it clear," he added, "that this is not a loss of control."

The analyst met his eyes. "What is it, then?"

Redding looked back at the screen—the clean edge, the calm ground, the water that had decided to stay where it was.

"It's a jurisdictional issue," he said. "And we will treat it as such."

No one moved to contradict him.

But as the screens dimmed and the room returned to its windowless quiet, it was already clear that the line of authority—like every other line—had begun to stop where it was no longer recognized.

CHAPTER ELEVEN

FRACTURE

Day 18

Dr. Elise Halvorsen was not supposed to be looking for patterns.

Her role—officially—was verification. Atmospheric stability. Post-event normalization. She was brought in after systems finished misbehaving, not while they were still deciding what they were.

She noticed the anomaly because it was too precise.

It appeared in a dataset she almost didn't open—an automated atmospheric comparison flagged by software designed to catch instrument drift, not meaning. The alert was minor, buried beneath dozens of others, and would normally have been cleared without comment.

Instead, Elise paused.

The Passer corridor outside Flagstaff had stabilized faster than the model allowed. Not dramatically. Not enough to trip alarms. Just enough to be wrong in a way that suggested intention rather than error.

She leaned closer to her screen.

Air particulate counts behind the corridor had dropped sharply—expected. Nitrogen oxides had normalized—expected. What wasn't expected was how clean the curve looked. No overshoot. No rebound. No oscillation. The system had not corrected itself. It had arrived.

Elise opened a second window and pulled soil composition readings from the same corridor. The samples had been taken less than six hours after the Passer passed through.

The soil was dark, uniform, and structurally sound in ways that defied normal formation timelines. Microbial activity had already stabilized. Not spiked. Not surged. Balanced.

She felt a familiar tightening behind her eyes—the sensation she associated with seeing something that would be explained away by everyone else.

"This isn't remediation," she murmured. "This is configuration."

Her phone buzzed.

A message from Margaret Liu, brief and carefully neutral.

You seeing this too?

Elise typed back immediately.

Yes. And it's not random.

She pulled up comparative data from three other corridors—Nevada, coastal Chile, southern Australia. The pattern held. Minor variation within narrow tolerances. Each corridor different, but compliant.

As if the system allowed for local conditions without relinquishing control.

Elise leaned back in her chair and closed her eyes.

She had seen this shape before.

Not in data—but in drawings.

She stood and crossed the room to a filing cabinet she had not opened in years. The metal drawer stuck slightly, protesting the interruption. Inside were scanned field notes from a coastal culture dismissed by mainstream archaeology as pre-symbolic.

No monuments.

No metallurgy.

No written language.

Just marks.

She spread the scans across her desk.

The images showed stones and bone fragments etched with wide, deliberate arcs—not decorative, not symmetrical. Lines ran parallel for long distances, then diverged without flourish. Some markings crossed rivers and shorelines without acknowledging them, continuing across boundaries that later cultures treated as meaningful.

There were no figures.

No animals.

No symbols that could be named.

Only paths.

Elise remembered where they had been found.

Wind-scoured headlands. River mouths that no longer existed. Raised beaches far inland, exposed only after long retreating waterlines. The artifacts never appeared deep in settlements. They were found at edges—places people passed through rather than stayed.

The culture itself had no name anyone agreed on. The sites were scattered across continents that should not have shared language, let alone practice. The dates refused to line up neatly. Each discovery had been explained in isolation, then quietly shelved when broader patterns threatened to emerge.

What united them was restraint.

In several drawings, the arcs were paired with narrow bands—consistent in width, too consistent to be incidental. The bands cut through clusters of smaller markings without interacting with them, as if the carver had been recording something that passed through a place rather than belonging to it.

The carvings did not dramatize.

They did not warn.

They did not celebrate.

They recorded.

The marks ended abruptly, often mid-stone, mid-bone, as though the maker had stopped not because the surface ran out, but because the event had moved beyond view.

At the time, the prevailing interpretation had been meta-phor—seasonal flooding, spiritual cycles, agricultural myth.

Elise had never accepted that.

She overlaid one of the scans with the satellite image of a modern corridor.

The alignment was not perfect.

Which was exactly what frightened her.

The ancient markings were less precise. Less controlled. As if they had been observed rather than executed. As if someone had tried to keep up, walking alongside something too large to understand, carving when they could, stopping when they couldn't.

Elise's pulse quickened.

"These aren't warnings," she said softly. "They're records."

Her phone buzzed again. This time it was a calendar alert.

INTER-AGENCY BRIEFING — 14:00

She almost dismissed it.

Instead, she opened a new document and began typing—not conclusions, not theories, just observations.

Upright motion

Edge-only contact

No compression

No debris

Rapid stabilization

Localized ecological balance

She stopped, fingers hovering.

What was missing wasn't data.

It was context.

Elise turned back to the scans and found a translated phrase written repeatedly in the margins by a long-dead hand, recorded centuries later by someone who did not understand it.

The ground passes.

The ground becomes.

We move aside.

She swallowed.

The Passers were not arriving.

They were continuing something.

Her phone vibrated again—this time a call.

Unknown secure number.

She answered.

"Dr. Halvorsen," a male voice said. Calm. Controlled.

"This is General Marcus Redding."

Elise did not respond immediately.

"I've been advised you're seeing patterns others aren't," Redding continued. "I'd like you on the briefing."

"That's not what you want," Elise said finally.

A pause.

"Tell me why," Redding said.

"Because once I say this out loud," she replied, "it stops being data and starts being language."

Another pause. Longer this time.

"Say it anyway," Redding said.

Elise looked at the corridor image still glowing faintly on her screen. At the dark, orderly ground behind it. At the clean, impossible boundary where a city had ended without breaking.

"These aren't destructive events," she said. "They're procedural."

"Procedural toward what?"

Elise closed her eyes.

"Toward something that doesn't include us as a variable."

Silence filled the line—not disbelief, but recalibration.

"Be at the briefing," Redding said at last. "And Dr. Halvorsen?"

"Yes?"

"Don't soften it."

The call ended.

Elise remained seated, staring at the data until the numbers stopped looking like abstractions and began to feel like pressure.

Outside her office window, the city continued—traffic lights cycling, pedestrians crossing streets that still existed, conversations about ordinary things.

Somewhere beyond the horizon, a Passer rolled forward at a pace no one needed to run from.

And for the first time since the disks emerged, Elise understood the real danger.

Not invasion.

Not extinction.

Meaning.

She gathered her notes, shut down her workstation, and stood.

Whatever this was, it had been here before.

And humanity, she suspected, was not its first audience.

CHAPTER TWELVE

DRIFT

Day 21

By the time the first national advisories expired, no one expected clarity to follow.

The language softened instead. Ongoing assessment. Evolving conditions. Localized impacts. Words that implied motion while avoiding direction. The Passers continued their slow advance through everything the statements carefully did not name.

In the corridors left behind, measurements stabilized.

Soil samples taken from the earliest paths showed consistency across continents—composition that didn't match any known terrestrial baseline, yet supported growth immediately. Not invasive species. Not aggressive proliferation. The vegetation that emerged behaved as if it had always belonged there, unfolding at a pace that suggested patience rather than urgency.

This was noted.

It was cataloged.

In places where the Passers had not yet arrived, people

waited for definition.

Some stayed because the maps said they could. Boundary projections still stopped short of their addresses. The shaded risk zones ended neatly, confidently, just beyond their streets. Leaving felt premature. Staying felt reasonable.

The notice arrived in the morning and said the house was still habitable.

The word appeared twice.

The door no longer closed properly unless lifted slightly. Water ran toward the wrong corner of the sink, not fast enough to alarm, just enough to notice once you were paying attention. A picture frame slid from the wall overnight without breaking. The nail remained firmly in place.

By noon, the backyard ended.

The grass beyond the fence stopped early, trimmed flat in a way no mower could achieve. The shed was missing its back half. Tools remained mounted inside, halved cleanly— rake handles ending in perfect circles, a ladder rung cut flush. Sawdust lay undisturbed on the floor, its edge sharp enough to trace with a finger.

Inside the house, the staircase stopped at the seventh step.

Above it, there was nothing. No landing. No debris. Just open air where the rest of the stairs should have continued. The cut was exact. The wood grain at the edge smooth and uninterrupted.

At 14:17, the notice updated.

**OCCUPANCY PERMITTED — PENDING REAS-
SESSMENT.**

Packing took less time than expected. Not because there

was little to take, but because the house had already begun to decide what still made sense. Rooms that remained intact felt provisional, like sets awaiting revision. Sunlight poured in through open planes where walls had been, warm and ordinary.

Before leaving, the door was locked.

The lock accepted the gesture without resistance.

From the street, the house looked almost normal. The façade remained intact. Curtains drawn. Windows unbroken. Only if you walked around the side could you see where the structure stopped—cut cleanly through bedrooms, closets, the shared assumption of interior space.

By evening, the address was no longer listed as residential.

It appeared instead as boundary-adjacent structure—still standing, still visible, but not recommended for approach.

This, too, was noted.

This, too, was cataloged.

Across agencies, language continued to adjust. Habitable became conditionally accessible. Unaffected became not yet engaged. No one announced when drift became the default condition. It simply arrived, and remained.

The Passers did not accelerate.

They did not slow.

They moved on, leaving behind corridors where growth stabilized, systems quieted, and homes ended without violence—finished precisely where they no longer applied.

By the end of the third week, most people understood what drift meant.

It was not confusion.

It was accommodation.

CHAPTER THIRTEEN

INTERPRETATION

Week 4

Caleb Marsh noticed the shift before anyone named it.

People began arriving early.

Not rushing. Not anxious. Just present—standing in small clusters outside the church before the doors opened, before the lights were on, before he had decided what he was going to say. They waited with the patience of people who believed something would begin whether or not they were told it had.

That unsettled him more than fear ever had.

Caleb had not always preached in rooms this small.

There had been a time when his sermons were streamed, clipped, quoted. When attendance numbers were tracked weekly and donors used phrases like reach and impact without irony. He had learned early how to shape uncertainty into language that felt like guidance, how to let people leave believing they had been steadied rather than persuaded.

He had been very good at it.

Caleb had once preached to crowds ten times this size and trusted himself less then than he did now. Back then, certainty had been the currency. The louder the promise, the fuller the seats. He knew how to land a phrase so it stayed with people for days, how to let silence feel intentional instead of empty.

That was why he left.

The scandal that followed had not been his, exactly. He had not lied. He had not stolen. He had not broken any law anyone could prove. What he had done was quieter and harder to defend: he had stayed silent when spectacle replaced care, when belief became product, when doubt was edited out of sermons because it tested poorly.

He told himself he had been protecting the congregation.

Later, he admitted he had been protecting himself.

This church was supposed to be different. Smaller. Temporary. A place where answers were not promised in advance. A place where attention could gather without becoming authority.

Now the sanctuary filled again.

People stood shoulder to shoulder, packed into pews and aisles, spilling out into the vestibule. Some sat on the floor. Some leaned against walls. No one complained. No one checked the time.

They had not come for explanation.

They had come because the Passer would cross nearby in three days, and no one knew how to talk about that yet.

Caleb waited until the room settled itself.

"My friends," he said gently, "I'm not here to explain anything to you."

The room exhaled.

"I'm here because something has passed through our

lives," he continued. "And we're still here to talk about it."

He could feel it immediately—the way the crowd leaned in without moving. He hated that part. The ease of it. The way attention obeyed him even when he asked nothing of it.

As if he were sitting in the back row of his own church, watching himself speak.

"You've all seen the footage," he said. "Cities cut cleanly. People moving aside. The ground afterward."

He did not say destruction.

He did not say death.

"They're calling them the Passers now," Caleb said, testing the word aloud. "Like that. It doesn't tell us what they are. It tells us what they do."

A ripple moved through the room.

"Everything that matters in this world passes," he said. "Bodies. Empires. Grief."

He stopped himself before finishing the thought the way he once would have.

"The question isn't whether we can stop them," he said softly. "The question is whether we trust what comes after."

Someone near the front began to cry, quietly, as if embarrassed by the sound.

Caleb folded his hands.

"I'm not telling anyone to stay," he said. "I'm not telling anyone to leave. I'm saying this: some of you already know where you're supposed to be."

The room felt closer now—not louder, just more focused.

"We've been trained our whole lives to run from change," he said. "To treat it as punishment. But what if this—" he gestured, encompassing the Passers, the moment, the waiting "—isn't about us at all?"

That was the line.

He felt it land and wished he could pull it back.

After the gathering ended, people didn't leave right away.

They lined up to speak with him. They thanked him. They asked where the Passer would be in three days, in five, in a week. They asked whether prayer mattered. Whether proximity mattered. Whether staying was dangerous.

Caleb listened.

He answered very little.

Late that night, long after the last car left the parking lot, he sat alone in his office with the lights off. The room smelled faintly of old paper and coffee. His phone lay face down on the desk.

He knew exactly how dangerous the day had been.

He had felt the crowd respond not to belief, but to permission. The release of being allowed not to decide yet. He had once built a career on that sensation.

Caleb opened a blank post and typed carefully.

Remain where you are, if you can.

The Passing is not an enemy.

Witness is enough.

He stared at the words for a long time.

Then he posted them.

Almost immediately, the notifications began.

Caleb turned the phone face down and knelt beside his chair—not to pray for answers, but to ask for restraint.

Outside, somewhere beyond the building and the quiet parking lot, a Passer continued its slow approach.

And Caleb Marsh wondered whether he was strong enough to let it pass without making himself essential.

CHAPTER FOURTEEN

PRESSURE

Week 4

The first coordinated attempt to interfere with a Passer occurred without ceremony.

It was not announced publicly. There were no speeches, no countdowns. A small operations unit was deployed under a classification that technically no longer existed, toward a Passer moving inland through unincorporated land that had once been farmland and had not yet been redefined.

The objective was modest.

Confirm material properties.

Test resistance.

Extract a surface sample if possible.

The Passer did not acknowledge their presence.

From a distance, it remained exactly what it had been—upright, matte, and slowly advancing, its mile-wide edge maintaining a contact line so clean it looked conceptual. No heat signatures. No electromagnetic distortion. No sound beyond wind passing around something too large to interrupt it.

The team approached from the side, careful to remain

outside the projected boundary. Their equipment registered nothing that could be meaningfully calibrated. Readings fluctuated within tolerances that assumed a world still operating under known constraints.

When they moved closer, the Passer continued to roll.

At a distance of fifty meters, one technician halted and signaled back. Not fear—confusion. The surface of the disk resisted visual fixation. Not because it shimmered or reflected, but because it offered no points of reference. The eye slid off it, unable to anchor scale or texture.

Attempts to drill were abandoned almost immediately. The bit made contact and failed—not snapping, not dulling, simply refusing to engage. Pressure increased. The drill registered torque without progress. The surface did not deform.

A cutting laser produced no measurable effect.

The Passer rolled forward.

The team adjusted position repeatedly, recalculating approach vectors that became irrelevant as the disk advanced with unbroken patience. Eventually, they retreated—not under threat, but under the recognition that nothing they did registered as interaction.

Later reports would describe the encounter as inconclusive.

What those reports did not capture was the moment of realization shared among the team as they withdrew: the sense that the Passer had not resisted them.

It had not needed to.

As the unit pulled back to a safe distance, the corridor behind the Passer darkened and settled. The soil appeared intact, structured, and already receptive to growth. No trace of interference remained—not from the landscape, and not from the humans who had attempted to interrupt it.

The Passer continued inland.

No escalation followed.

No second attempt was authorized.

The event passed into briefing slides and restricted memos, stripped of its texture and filed as non-actionable.

On the ground, the land continued to reorganize itself.

And somewhere between observation and withdrawal, it became clear that the Passers did not distinguish between interference and irrelevance.

They moved through both without alteration.

CHAPTER FIFTEEN

ATTRIBUTION

Month 4

The first injury happened quietly.

A man slipped while crossing the corridor boundary near Bakersfield—lost his footing on the new soil where asphalt had ended without warning. He fell hard, broke his wrist, stood up embarrassed, and laughed while others helped him to his feet.

The footage barely circulated.

It wasn't violent enough to outrage anyone.

It wasn't symbolic enough to be shared.

It didn't fit a narrative.

Which is why it mattered.

By the end of the week, similar incidents followed. Minor. Accidental. A twisted ankle here. A delivery truck that misjudged the firmness of the ground and sank just enough to require towing. A cyclist who crossed the boundary at speed and went down hard, blood bright against the dark soil.

No one blamed the Passers.

They blamed confusion.

Local governments began installing temporary barriers—

cones, tape, portable fencing—anything to mark the line that could not be seen from a distance. None of it lasted long. The soil behind the Passers did not resist removal, but it did not accept structures easily either. Posts leaned. Anchors loosened. Fences came down overnight.

It was as if the ground rejected permanence.

Elise Halvorsen stood at the edge of the Flagstaff corridor with a portable scanner humming quietly at her side. The air was cool. Too clean. Her lungs noticed the difference before her instruments did.

"This isn't erosion," she said to no one in particular. "It's refusal."

A technician beside her frowned. "Refusal of what?"

Elise knelt and pressed her palm flat against the soil.

"Refusal of imprint," she said. "It doesn't want to hold what was here."

The soil was firm beneath her hand—supportive, stable—but it did not accept pressure the way ordinary ground did. When she lifted her palm, there was no print.

Behind her, a small group watched silently. Stayers. Observers. People who had stopped asking permission to be present.

A woman stepped forward. "Is it dangerous?"

Elise stood.

"It's not hostile," she said. "But it's not accommodating."

That answer spread faster than the data.

Across social platforms, a phrase began to appear.

The ground won't keep us.

At first it was poetic. Then it became logistical.

Property disputes followed almost immediately. Deeds referenced coordinates that no longer connected to anything recognizable. Surveyors argued over whether land that had been replaced could still be owned. Insurance companies quietly revised their exclusions.

In one county, a judge ruled that the corridor constituted an act of reclassification, not destruction. The ruling was appealed within hours.

General Redding received the summary late at night.

He read it without expression.

This was the phase he had feared—not panic, not violence, but ambiguity hardening into policy.

He opened a secure channel.

"Update the guidance," he said. "Corridor boundaries are to be treated as unstable terrain."

"Sir," an aide replied, "that will effectively freeze development across—"

"I know," Redding said. "That's the point."

"But the economic impact—"

"—was already happening," Redding finished. "This just names it."

When the call ended, Redding remained seated, staring at the quiet feed from a corridor camera somewhere in the Midwest.

A group of people stood near the boundary, talking softly. One of them stepped forward experimentally, placed a foot on the new soil, shifted weight, then stepped back.

They laughed.

Not because it was funny—but because it was strange, and laughter was still allowed.

That night, Caleb Marsh received an email he did not open right away.

It was from someone he recognized. Someone with credentials. Someone asking him to clarify whether his language implied endorsement of permanent settlement within the corridors.

Caleb closed the message and set the phone down.

He walked outside instead.

The Passer near the city was visible now—closer than it had been the day before, though only just. Its movement could only be measured by commitment to watching it long enough to notice change.

Caleb stood with his hands in his pockets and felt the weight of what he had helped create.

Not belief.

Expectation.

The ground behind the Passer was dark and clean, stretching away like an invitation that refused to explain itself.

Caleb wondered, not for the first time, whether meaning arrived after events—or whether humans simply rushed to fill silence before it could decide for itself.

Far away, unseen, another minor incident occurred.

A temporary barrier failed.

A person stumbled.

And somewhere in a system already stretched thin, a checkbox was marked.

The world had not broken.

But it had begun, almost imperceptibly, to misalign.

CHAPTER SIXTEEN

MISUSE

Month 5

The corridor had been open long enough to develop routines.

At first, access was restricted—temporary fencing, monitoring stations, signage that warned without explaining. But as the Passer moved on and the transformed land stabilized, those boundaries softened. Gates were moved. Barriers were repositioned. Eventually, they were removed altogether.

People entered cautiously at first.

They stepped from intact ground onto the darkened soil as if testing ice. Some knelt. Some pressed their palms flat against the surface, expecting warmth or vibration and finding neither. The soil was cool, fine-grained, and unexpectedly resilient underfoot.

Nothing resisted them.

Nothing welcomed them either.

Within days, footpaths appeared—not imposed, but worn by repetition. Individuals returned alone, then in pairs. Researchers followed, setting markers that were quietly ignored or displaced. Children crossed the corridor without pause, chasing one another across land their parents still hesitated to touch.

The vegetation remained restrained.

Thin green filaments rose evenly, never choking, never overrunning. Growth followed no familiar pattern, yet it did not compete. It occupied space as if the space had been waiting.

The air changed closer to the center.

Not dramatically—no gust, no pressure shift—but a subtle clarity that made breathing feel deliberate rather than automatic. The smell arrived with it, faint but unmistakable. Clean rain. Not recent rain, not wet earth, but the memory of rain after heat, after dust. A freshness that didn't belong to weather so much as reset.

People noticed without remarking on it.

They lingered longer than planned. Sat without checking time. Conversations softened, then trailed off entirely, as if the corridor absorbed excess intention along with sound.

Elise watched from the perimeter during one of the first unregulated crossings.

She had been invited to speak, to contextualize, to offer language that would slow behavior by explaining it. She declined. Explanation, she suspected, would arrive too late.

A man walked past her carrying a folding chair. He stopped near the center of the corridor and unfolded it carefully, facing the direction the Passer had gone. He sat, hands resting on his knees, and remained there long after others drifted away.

No one told him to move.

No one told him to stay.

The corridor absorbed sound. Voices carried poorly. Even wind seemed altered, bending low across the surface before lifting again at the far edge.

Data streams continued to confirm what observation already suggested: air quality within the corridor measured marginally higher than surrounding regions. Water samples collected from runoff showed reduced contaminants without filtration. The changes were incremental, almost modest—but they persisted.

No decay was observed.

By the end of the week, informal markets had begun to appear along the corridor's edge. Not commerce—exchange. Tools for produce. Labor for access. People lingered longer than necessity required, leaving only when reminded by schedules that no longer felt binding.

Municipal authorities issued guidance recommending limited exposure.

Compliance was uneven.

The corridor did not respond.

At night, the transformed land reflected less ambient light than the city around it, creating a soft absence that resisted illumination. From a distance, it looked like a missing strip of world, quietly refusing the patterns projected onto it.

Elise stood with General Redding near a temporary observation post, watching as people crossed freely between what had been and what now existed.

"This isn't panic," Redding said.

"No," Elise replied.

"It's not devotion either."

"No."

He waited.

Elise's gaze followed a group walking slowly across the corridor, their conversation muted by the soil beneath them.

"It's practice," she said. "They're learning where they can stand."

Behind them, beyond the corridor, the city continued with strained normalcy—traffic redirected, schedules adjusted, maps redrawn.

Ahead of them, in the direction the Passer had gone, the land remained unmarked.

The process did not ask permission.

It did not enforce participation.

It simply left space.

And people, Elise realized, were beginning to step into it without waiting to be told what it meant.

CHAPTER SEVENTEEN

ESCALATION

Month 6

The first unauthorized operation began as a favor.

A regional commander approved a request to deploy a small engineering team near a corridor in eastern Oregon—ostensibly to assess soil stability for emergency access routes. The paperwork was clean. The language was cautious. The team was told not to interfere.

They brought instruments anyway.

The Passer had crossed the river two days earlier, leaving behind a mile-wide band of dark ground that cut through pine forest and farmland with surgical calm. The corridor looked quiet from a distance. Orderly. Like something that had finished its work.

The team set up at dawn.

They wore standard protective gear—helmets, respirators, biometric monitors—more for optics than necessity. The air was clear. Too clear. Sound carried strangely, as if the land had forgotten how to echo.

"Baseline readings only," the team lead said. "We don't

touch the edge."

They didn't mean to.

But the boundary was hard to see unless you stood still long enough for your eyes to adjust. Asphalt ended. Soil began. No warning. No debris. No sense of transition beyond a subtle change in color and texture.

One of the engineers stepped forward to adjust a tripod.

His boot crossed the line.

Nothing happened.

He froze, heart racing, then laughed—relief flooding his face.

"I'm fine," he said. "It's solid."

The others watched him carefully as he shifted his weight, testing the ground. It held. Supported him. Offered no resistance, but no collapse either.

"Careful," someone said.

He nodded and stepped back across the boundary.

That was the moment the decision changed.

If it could be crossed.

If it could be stood on.

If nothing happened—

Then perhaps something could be done.

They moved closer.

Not all at once. One at a time. Each step tentative. Each success reinforcing the last. Instruments were placed. Samples taken. A core drill was unpacked.

"Just a shallow bore," the team lead said. "For composition."

The drill bit touched the soil.

The motor whined.

Then stalled.

Not from resistance—but from nothing to bite into. The soil did not compress, fracture, or shear. The bit spun uselessly, as if pressed against an idea rather than a surface.

The engineer pulled back, confused.

"Try again," the lead said.

They increased torque.

The drill stopped completely.

Alarms chimed softly as systems registered unexpected load without mechanical engagement.

"Power down," the lead said.

Too late.

The drill housing cracked—not violently, not explosively. It simply separated, components loosening as if their fasteners had never been tightened. The drill fell apart in pieces at their feet.

Silence followed.

The engineer stared at his hands.

"I didn't feel anything," he said. "It didn't push back."

Behind them, one of the monitors spiked.

Heart rate. Cortisol. Neural stress indicators—all rising without corresponding physical cause.

"Everyone step back," the lead ordered.

They retreated across the boundary.

The readings normalized within seconds.

No one spoke.

They packed up without discussion.

The report that followed was heavily qualified. No damage to personnel. No anomalous energy release. Equipment failure attributed to design flaw pending further review.

It was signed, routed, and quietly buried.

Except it wasn't.
Within hours, copies appeared in adjacent command systems. Then in foreign intelligence briefs. Then—stripped of context—online.
They tried to drill it.
The ground refused.
The phrase spread faster than any official correction.
General Redding received the alert mid-briefing.
"Who authorized this?" he asked.
No one answered.
"That's not a rhetorical question," he said.
An aide cleared her throat. "It appears to have been approved at a regional level. Classified as non-interactive."
Redding closed his eyes.
The problem was no longer belief.
It was curiosity armed with resources.
He ended the briefing early and placed a call.
"Elise," he said when she answered. "They touched it."
A pause.
"Did it respond?" she asked.
"No," Redding said. "That's worse."
Elise looked at the data as it arrived—equipment failure logs, biometric traces, environmental readings that showed nothing where something should have been.
"They didn't hit a wall," she said quietly. "They hit a condition."
"What kind?"
"One that assumes you're not supposed to be there."
That night, footage surfaced from a different corridor—

grainy, unverified, but compelling.

A group stood at the boundary with a makeshift rig. Not military. Not official. Just determined.

They believed the Passers were indifferent.

They believed indifference meant permission.

The video cut out just as the device made contact.

No explosion followed.

No sound.

Just the camera dropping, frame tilting toward the dark soil.

The last thing visible was the boundary line—perfectly intact.

By morning, advisories escalated.

NO CONTACT WITH PASSER CORRIDORS
UNAUTHORIZED INTERACTION
STRICTLY PROHIBITED

The language was firmer now.

Too late.

The world had crossed from waiting into testing.

And testing, once begun, rarely stayed controlled.

CHAPTER EIGHTEEN

FRAMING

Month 6

The mistake was not arrogance.

It was familiarity.

By the sixth month, the Passers had been mapped, modeled, narrated, and named. Their paths were predictable in the narrow sense that mattered to logistics. Their speed had been measured down to the hour. Their behavior—or lack of it—had been cataloged exhaustively.

They did not react.

They did not resist.

They did not respond.

That consistency bred a dangerous assumption: that absence of response meant absence of boundary.

The team in southern Arizona believed this.

They were not military. They were not unaffiliated amateurs either. They were contractors—experienced, credentialed, operating under a patchwork authorization that looked legitimate if you didn't ask too many questions.

Their goal was modest: test whether a temporary structure

could be erected within the corridor, behind the Passer's path. A platform. A walkway. Something removable. Something that would prove the land could be used.

They arrived early, before heat shimmered the air.

The corridor stretched ahead of them—dark, clean soil framed by untouched desert. The Passer itself was miles away now, already past the point of interest. What remained looked calm. Stable.

Inviting, in a way no one liked admitting.

They placed the first support post carefully.

It sank into the soil without resistance.

No cracking.

No deformation.

No feedback at all.

"That's good," one of them said. "It's taking the load."

They placed a second post.

Then a third.

The structure began to take shape—lightweight, modular, designed to be dismantled quickly if needed.

When the first section of decking went down, they stepped onto it cautiously.

Nothing happened.

Laughter followed—not relief this time, but triumph.

"See?" someone said. "It's fine."

They didn't notice the problem immediately.

It appeared first in the instruments.

Load distribution readings flattened—too flat. Stress values failed to register gradients. The platform wasn't bearing weight so much as existing in a state where weight had no meaning.

"That's odd," the engineer murmured.

He stepped back onto the decking to recalibrate the sensor.

The platform did not collapse.

It did not tilt or shift.

It simply ceased to be where it was.

There was no sound.

No visible displacement.

One moment, the man was standing mid-step.

The next, he wasn't.

The decking behind him remained intact. The support posts still stood. The air closed quietly.

Someone screamed his name.

Another ran forward, stopping just short of the place where he had been.

There was no crater.

No blood.

No sign that anything had passed through.

The soil beneath the gap was smooth, uninterrupted, indistinguishable from the rest of the corridor.

As if the person had never occupied that position.

The remaining crew backed away slowly, hands raised—not toward anything in particular, but away from the absence where their colleague should have been.

Emergency services arrived too late to be useful.

The official report would later describe the incident as a catastrophic spatial discontinuity resulting in presumed fatality.

Unofficial footage told a simpler story.

A man stepped where something did not permit standing.

General Redding received the call while reviewing evacuation models that no longer mattered.

He listened without interrupting.

"Was there resistance?" he asked when the report ended.

"No, sir."

"Any warning?"

"No."

Redding closed his eyes.

"This wasn't a breach," he said. "It was a misread."

Elise Halvorsen watched the footage once.

She did not watch it again.

"They keep thinking the ground is passive," she said to no one. "It isn't hostile—but it isn't inert."

She wrote a single line in her notes and underlined it twice.

The corridor is not a place. It is a state.

By evening, the story had spread everywhere.

The language hardened.

Absorbed.

Taken.

Claimed.

People argued online about what had happened, whether the man had been destroyed or transformed or relocated. Some insisted the Passers were selective. Others claimed it was punishment.

A smaller group said nothing at all.

They simply stopped going near the corridors.

In one city, a vigil formed—not at the boundary, but at a distance where the Passer was visible without inviting proximity. No speeches. No signs. Just people standing quietly, acknowledging something they did not understand.

The Passer continued its slow movement elsewhere, unaffected.

Behind it, the ground remained dark, clean, and silent.

Ahead of it, humanity lost the last illusion that indifference meant safety.

CHAPTER NINETEEN

ENFORCEMENT

Month 7

The models stopped agreeing shortly after the fourth week.

Not failing—disagreeing.

Simulations that shared inputs diverged without error, producing outcomes that could not be reconciled through revision or recalibration. Analysts flagged the discrepancy and received no guidance on how to proceed. There was no protocol for models that behaved as if the future itself refused convergence.

The Passers continued to move.

Their paths, once plotted as isolated trajectories, began to suggest relationships that were difficult to define without overstating. No two disks intersected. No two slowed for the presence of another. Yet their distribution across the planet formed patterns that held regardless of scale.

Large arcs repeated inside smaller ones.

Distances that should have been arbitrary were not.

The realization arrived without announcement: the Passers were not independent objects sharing a surface.

They were components.

This interpretation circulated quietly, stripped of adjectives. It did not require consensus to persist. Those who encountered it tended to stop arguing against it, not because it was convincing, but because alternatives demanded more effort to maintain.

Elise encountered the revised projections late at night, alone in a borrowed office whose walls still carried the outlines of removed displays. She studied the overlays without attempting to simplify them. The shapes held whether she named them or not.

What unsettled her was not the coherence.

It was the absence of optimization.

The Passers did not appear to be correcting damage, or targeting failure points, or maximizing efficiency by any human metric. Their movement did not prioritize population density or ecological collapse. Cities were crossed as readily as open land. Polluted regions were not favored over pristine ones.

Nothing about the pattern suggested urgency.

Which implied time.

Elsewhere, secondary effects continued to accumulate without coordination. Weather systems shifted subtly along corridor boundaries. Migration patterns adjusted in advance of the Passers' arrival, as if responding to a pressure gradient that instruments could not register.

Attempts to model causality stalled.

The question of intent receded again—not disproven, simply irrelevant to prediction.

In one internal briefing, the Passers were described as distributed infrastructure undergoing phased activation. The phrase survived two rounds of revision before being removed for tone. It continued to appear in handwritten notes afterward.

Elise closed the file without saving annotations.

She understood now why the earliest myths she had studied resisted narrative resolution. The language was wrong. Stories assumed agency where there was only function.

The Passers did not move toward anything.

They moved through.

The distinction mattered.

Outside the office window, the city continued its altered rhythm—rerouted traffic, provisional structures, people learning where to stand. Normality persisted not as restoration, but as accommodation.

Elise gathered her things and left the building without turning off the lights.

The future was no longer something to be extrapolated.

It was something already underway, unfolding at a scale that made agreement unnecessary.

CHAPTER TWENTY

INTERVENTION

Month 8

The first adaptations were small enough to feel clever.

A city rerouted traffic around a corridor that cut through its western districts, repainting lanes overnight and congratulating itself on the speed of response. A farming cooperative shifted irrigation lines to draw from runoff that pooled along the corridor's edge, reporting improved yields without explanation.

"These are interim measures," officials said. "Stopgaps."

But stopgaps had a way of becoming permanent when nothing contradicted them.

In Kansas, a logistics firm began testing modular bridges designed to span corridor zones without touching the soil behind the Passers. Lightweight. Suspended. Fully removable. The first installation went up in twelve hours.

It worked.

Trucks crossed. Sensors registered no anomalies. The bridge did not sag or drift. The soil beneath it remained unchanged.

The footage went viral.

Adaptation is possible, someone wrote.

We don't have to surrender.

General Redding watched the clip in silence.

"Who approved this?" he asked.

"No one," an aide replied. "It's classified as civilian infra-structure."

Redding nodded slowly.

That was the problem.

Across the Atlantic, a coastal city began marketing newly stabilized corridor land as a public green way—no permanent structures, no digging, just foot traffic and temporary instal-lations. The air was cleaner. The soil held. Visitors reported improved sleep, reduced respiratory symptoms.

"This is coexistence," the mayor said at a press event. "Not resistance."

Elise Halvorsen stood in the crowd, listening.

She did not argue.

Instead, she waited.

Her data was beginning to show second-order effects— minor deviations in corridor behavior that didn't break pattern but nudged it. A fraction of a degree in curvature. A slight delay in stabilization time.

Nothing anyone else would notice.

Yet.

"These aren't failures," she said later to a small group of analysts. "They're accommodations."

"Isn't that good?" one asked.

Elise shook her head.

"Accommodation implies negotiation," she said. "And

negotiation implies recognition."

She pulled up a comparative overlay—ancient markings beside modern corridors.

"They didn't build on these paths," she said. "They moved around them. Always."

Someone laughed nervously.

"That was then," another said. "This is different."

Elise didn't respond.

Caleb Marsh watched the bridges appear online, the green ways, the headlines that framed adaptation as victory. He felt the familiar pressure of language hardening too quickly.

He drafted a message and did not post it.

Instead, he walked out toward the corridor near his city— not close, not testing limits, just far enough to feel the presence.

People were already there.

Not waiting now.

Using.

A woman practiced yoga on a mat laid just outside the boundary. A man read a book aloud to a small group seated on folding chairs. Children played tag, careful not to cross the invisible line.

No one seemed afraid.

That frightened him.

That night, Elise sent a memo she knew would be ignored.

PRELIMINARY OBSERVATION:

PASSER CORRIDORS EXHIBIT CONDITIONAL TOLERANCE, NOT STABILITY.

RECOMMENDATION: HALT ALL STRUCTURAL ADAPTATIONS PENDING LONG-TERM ANALYSIS.

The response was polite and dismissive.

Thank you for your insight.

We will incorporate this into the ongoing review.

By morning, three new projects had been announced.

The Passers continued moving.

They did not react to bridges, or foot traffic, or green ways. They did not acknowledge coexistence.

But the data showed something subtle.

Where adaptation clustered, the corridors grew fractionally less predictable.

Nothing dramatic.

Nothing immediate.

Just enough to suggest that the system was not passive.

It was observing.

And somewhere in the world's rush to live normally again, humanity mistook tolerance for permission.

CHAPTER TWENTY-ONE

FEEDBACK

Month 9

The first sign was not failure.

It was delay.

A Passer crossing the outskirts of Rotterdam slowed by six minutes.

Not enough to trigger alerts. Not enough to be visible without precise comparison. Just long enough for Elise Halvorsen to stop mid-sentence during a briefing and turn back to the screen.

"That's new," she said.

Someone chuckled. "Six minutes?"

Elise didn't smile.

Passers did not slow.

They did not hesitate. They did not modulate their pace in response to terrain, weather, or observation density. Their speed had varied only within margins that correlated perfectly with planetary curvature.

Until now.

She pulled up the corridor overlay. The delay coincided exactly with a zone of concentrated human adaptation—pedestrian traffic, temporary structures, suspended utilities. Nothing intrusive. Nothing violent.

Just presence.

"Correlation isn't causation," an analyst offered.

"Agreed," Elise said. "But repetition is."

By the end of the week, three more micro-delays appeared.

Six minutes.

Nine.

Fourteen.

Each near sites where adaptation had become normalized.

General Redding received the update with a tightening jaw.

"They're not reacting," he said over the secure line. "They're recalibrating."

"Yes," Elise replied. "Which means they're noticing."

That distinction spread quietly through command structures, stripped of nuance as it went.

The Passers respond.

They can be influenced.

Someone leaked the Rotterdam data.

The narrative flipped overnight.

Headlines shifted tone.

HUMAN ACTIVITY MAY AFFECT PASSER BEHAV-IORADAPTATION STRATEGIES SHOW PROMISE

A city council in South America voted unanimously to expand corridor use, framing it as participation rather than interference. A consortium announced plans to build mobile housing platforms designed to migrate alongside the Passers' paths.

"This is cooperation," the press release said.

Elise watched it all unfold with a growing sense of dread.

"They're not partners," she said to Redding during a late-night call. "They're processes."

"And processes don't like noise," Redding replied.

The cost arrived two days later.

A Passer in central Asia adjusted its path.

Not dramatically.

A fraction of a degree.

Enough to miss a previously projected corridor and clip the edge of a city that had been declared safe.

Evacuation orders had been relaxed there. Infrastructure projects had resumed. People had returned to buildings marked low-risk.

The Passer did not strike suddenly.

It arrived with its usual patience.

There was time to leave.

But there was not time to undo confidence.

A residential block vanished—replaced cleanly by dark soil and faint green growth. No collapse. No rubble. No explosion.

Just absence.

The footage was eerily calm.

People walking away in an orderly line. A woman stopping to retrieve a potted plant from a windowsill before remembering the window no longer existed.

The city survived.

Trust did not.

The correction orders were immediate and absolute.

All adaptation projects halted.

All corridor zones cleared.

All predictive models suspended.

Too late.

The damage was not the loss of buildings.

It was the realization that adaptation had introduced variability—and variability had introduced error.

Caleb Marsh watched the footage alone.

He had spoken carefully for months, choosing language that did not inflame or instruct. Now words felt irrelevant.

People wanted to believe they had been acknowledged.

They wanted to believe participation mattered.

What they had actually done was add friction to something that did not recognize intent.

That night, Elise wrote a single sentence in her notebook and underlined it twice.

The system tolerates us until it doesn't.

General Redding issued the most restrictive directive of his career the following morning.

—NO HUMAN PRESENCE WITHIN CORRIDOR ZONES—
—NO STRUCTURAL ADAPTATION—
—NO FURTHER EXPERIMENTATION—

The order would be followed.

For a while.

The Passers resumed their original pace.

As if nothing had happened.

But the world understood now that silence was not safety—and that feedback, once triggered, could not be unlearned.

Somewhere ahead, beyond any model's reach, consequences waited patiently.

Just like the Passers.

CHAPTER TWENTY-TWO

RESISTANCE

Month 10

The problem was not that the rules changed.

It was that they changed at different speeds.

After the Rotterdam correction, global directives hardened overnight. Corridor exclusion zones expanded. Military patrols appeared where none had been before. Access points were sealed with a seriousness that suggested regret more than authority.

In some places, the orders held.

In others, they unraveled almost immediately.

A coastal city in Southeast Asia ignored the clearance directive entirely, citing economic necessity. Fishing fleets continued to launch from waters now intersected by a Passer's projected path, skirting the corridor by meters. The Passer crossed anyway, water folding around its edge without disturbance.

The fishermen adapted.

They always had.

In Eastern Europe, a regional government declared corridor land heritage territory and refused to enforce removals. Monks returned to a valley that had been cut clean months earlier, ringing bells at dawn and dusk as the Passer advanced nearby.

No one stopped them.

In parts of the American Midwest, enforcement went the other direction. Armed checkpoints sprang up overnight. Families were turned away from homes that still stood but were deemed too close to future corridors. The language of safety hardened into the language of exclusion.

"This is temporary," officials said.

Temporary acquired a longer horizon than anyone admitted.

General Redding watched the reports stack up.

"What we have," he said to his staff, "is not a compliance problem."

He pointed to the screen, where maps pulsed with conflicting color codes.

"It's a synchronization problem."

Orders issued in Washington arrived too late in places where the Passers were already near. In other regions, they arrived too early—parking resistance where nothing had yet been lost.

People did what people always did when systems desynced.

They followed the version that felt most immediate.

Elise Halvorsen moved between briefings like a ghost.

Her warnings had not been wrong. They had simply arrived out of phase with belief.

"The corridors don't care about borders," she said repeatedly. "But people do."

In one meeting, an official snapped.

"Are you saying this is our fault?"

Elise shook her head.

"No," she said. "I'm saying it's our responsibility."

That distinction did not travel well.

Caleb Marsh saw the fracture from the ground.

Attendance at his gatherings dropped sharply—not because people had stopped believing, but because belief had splintered. Some stayed away out of fear. Others stayed away because they felt watched. A few arrived late at night, quietly, as if proximity itself had become suspect.

"Are we allowed to be here?" one man asked him.

Caleb did not answer immediately.

"Yes," he said finally. "But not without consequence."

That night, footage circulated of a confrontation near a corridor checkpoint. A woman refused to leave. A soldier raised his voice. The camera cut before anything irreversible occurred.

It didn't matter.

The image spread faster than context ever could.

They're choosing sides.

They're enforcing obedience.

They're protecting nothing.

The Passers continued moving.

In some regions, they became landmarks—unquestioned, integrated into daily life at a cautious distance. In others, they were treated as weapons by association, their paths surrounded by tension they neither caused nor absorbed.

The most destabilizing effect was not destruction.

It was inconsistency.

People could tolerate loss if it was shared.

They could tolerate rules if they were predictable.

What they could not tolerate was watching one city adapt peacefully while another cracked under force.

By the end of the month, the phrase corridor justice began appearing online, undefined but heavy with implication.

General Redding issued another directive—this one quieter than the last.

—DE-ESCALATION PRIORITY—
MINIMIZE FORCE IN ALL CORRIDOR OPERATIONS

He knew it would not be enough.

The Passers had revealed a truth no one liked confronting:

The world did not break all at once.

It broke unevenly.

And uneven breaks spread faster than clean ones ever could.

CHAPTER TWENTY-THREE

CONVERGENCE

Month 11

The first shots were not fired at a Passer.
They were fired near one.

The distinction mattered only to the people who made it.
The corridor outside Marseilles had been quiet for
weeks—a wide band of dark ground cutting inland from the
coast, flanked by temporary fencing and halfhearted patrols.
The Passer itself had already moved on, leaving behind land
that felt older than maps and newer than memory.
A group gathered there just after dusk.
They were not Stayers in the old sense. They did not bring
chairs or thermoses or quiet reverence. They arrived with
banners, cameras, and a clear intention to be seen.
"This land is not theirs," a woman shouted toward the
line of officers blocking the road. "It's not anyone's."
The officers held position.
Orders had changed twice that week.
First: hold the boundary.
Then: avoid escalation.

Then: enforce compliance.

No one had explained how to do all three at once.
The crowd pressed closer.
Someone crossed the invisible line.
Nothing happened.
That was enough.
An officer shouted. Another raised a rifle—not aimed at the crowd, but upward, into the air. The shot cracked across the corridor, sharp and final in a way nothing else had been.
Silence followed.
The Passer did not respond.
That image—armed authority firing near a corridor—spread globally within minutes.
Commentary split instantly.
Necessary control.
Unforgivable provocation.
Proof that the real danger was never the disks.
General Redding watched the footage with his jaw clenched.
"They panicked," an aide said.
"No," Redding replied. "They were confused."
That was worse.
He issued an immediate stand-down order to all corridor-adjacent units under his command.
It did not reach everyone in time.
In a city in Central America, police forcibly cleared a gathering near a corridor, using tear gas. The wind carried it back toward the officers instead, dispersing into the dark soil where it seemed to vanish without effect.
The crowd did not disperse.

They knelt.

The footage went viral.

Caleb Marsh saw it late that night.

He recognized the posture again—not reverence, not defiance, but surrender without submission. A refusal to perform fear in the expected way.

He wrote a single line on a scrap of paper and taped it above his desk.

If force arrives before meaning, meaning will flee.

Elise Halvorsen spent the night fielding calls she could not answer.

They wanted her to explain whether the Passers had caused this.

She told them the truth.

"No," she said. "They've only revealed where we disagree."

By morning, the term line breach appeared in official briefings—not referring to corridors, but to social ones.

Trust in enforcement fractured further. Compliance became conditional. People stopped asking what was allowed and began asking who was deciding.

The Passers continued their steady movement across the planet.

They did not acknowledge banners, bullets, or bodies kneeling at their boundaries.

Behind them, the ground remained unchanged.

Ahead of them, the human world pressed inward on itself, lines blurring between protection and control.

The breach had not occurred in the earth.

It had occurred in the story people were telling themselves about who was still in charge.

CHAPTER TWENTY-FOUR

SATURATION

Month 12

The term appeared first in an academic footnote.

Elise Halvorsen noticed it while reviewing a comparative translation from a coastal archive she had nearly forgotten— an annotation added centuries after the original markings were recorded, by someone trying to make sense of a pattern they could not alter.

The interval is not the passing.

It is the time we are given.

Elise sat back, the room suddenly too quiet.

Outside the briefing complex, the city moved with the careful normalcy that had settled over everything—traffic rerouted, schedules adjusted, conversations shortened. People spoke less about the Passers now, not because they mattered less, but because they had become part of the weather.

Predictable.

Indifferent.

Always there.

She brought the phrase to the next closed session.

Not as a theory.

As a frame.

"We've been asking the wrong question," she said to the room. "Not what are they doing? But what happens while they do it?"

A senior advisor frowned. "You're suggesting we stop responding."

"I'm suggesting we stop improvising," Elise replied. "There is a window—an interval—where systems can adjust without breaking. We are burning it on panic and proof-of-control."

The room resisted the idea at first. It sounded passive. Academic. Like surrender in clean language.

But Elise continued.

"The Passers don't accelerate," she said. "They don't correct for us. They don't acknowledge us at all. Which means the only variable left is how we behave during the time they give."

General Redding listened without interruption.

He had not slept well since Marseilles.

"This reframes authority," he said at last. "From enforcement to endurance."

"Yes," Elise said. "And endurance doesn't look decisive in the short term."

Redding nodded slowly.

"It looks weak," he said.

"But it isn't," Elise replied. "It's adaptive."

Outside government channels, the idea spread differently.

Not as policy.

As practice.

In cities where enforcement had failed, people began organizing schedules around the Passers' pace—moving markets seasonally, relocating schools in stages, designing temporary housing meant to dissolve and reform without attachment.

No protests.

No declarations.

Just adjustment.

In one region, a corridor cut through a manufacturing district. Rather than fight the loss, the city converted remaining facilities into mobile workshops—skills that traveled, labor that did not anchor itself to land that would not stay.

Caleb Marsh watched the change with cautious relief.

Attendance at his gatherings stabilized—not growing, not shrinking. People came not for answers, but for calibration. To sit together without instruction. To remember how to exist without insisting on meaning immediately.

He spoke less now.

Listened more.

People told stories instead—of moving houses twice in a year, of leaving jobs without resentment, of learning which things could be carried and which had to be released.

Not everyone adapted.

Some clung to control until it hurt.

But enough people learned the rhythm that panic no longer dominated the news cycle.

The Passers continued.

One year in, their paths had redrawn maps quietly. Borders mattered less than timing. Ownership mattered less than access. Permanence became a temporary concept.

The world had not healed.

But it had slowed its bleeding.

Elise stood at the edge of a corridor at dusk, watching the faint green growth behind the Passer catch the last light of the day.

"This isn't the end," she said softly.

No one argued.

The interval had never promised an ending.

Only time.

And for the first time since the disks emerged, humanity began—unevenly, imperfectly—to use it.

CHAPTER TWENTY-FIVE

CONTINUITY

Month 14

Time, once named, became something people tried to own.

The interval was never evenly distributed. That truth emerged slowly at first, then all at once.

Cities with resources adjusted schedules, moved infrastructure in phases, absorbed loss like a budget item. Cities without them improvised—sometimes brilliantly, sometimes disastrously. Rural corridors emptied faster than urban ones. Coastal paths were abandoned with less argument than inland crossings where land had been held for generations.

Maps began to appear online—unofficial, collaborative, constantly revised.

Safe until Month 18.

Projected displacement window.

Last viable harvest.

They were shared like weather forecasts. Like warnings. Like bets.

Governments attempted to formalize the process.

It sounded humane.
It felt arbitrary.

In one region, hospital wards were moved twice in six months, patients transferred in rolling convoys that became familiar sights on highways. In another, a school district closed early for the year, converting classrooms into temporary housing for families who had nowhere else to go.

People began to talk about running out of interval.

Not metaphorically.

Literally.

A community meeting in northern Italy ended in shouting when residents learned their relocation window had been shortened by three weeks to accommodate an industrial facility deemed "economically essential."

"Essential to whom?" someone demanded.

No one answered.

Caleb Marsh received a letter written by hand.

It was careful. Polite. Asking whether his gatherings could host mediation sessions—space for people whose schedules no longer aligned to speak before decisions were finalized.

He agreed before finishing the letter.

They sat in circles. They brought calendars. They argued quietly. No one won.

But they left less angry.

Elise Halvorsen watched allocation models fracture under their own assumptions.

They treated time like space—divisible, transferable, controllable.

It wasn't.

"The interval isn't a resource," she said during a briefing. "It's a condition."

Someone scoffed.

"Tell that to people who have to move next month."

"I am," Elise replied. "That's why this is failing."

The first coordinated refusal occurred shortly after.

A mid-sized city in South America rejected its relocation timetable outright. Officials cited public health data, local adaptation success, and—quietly—the belief that the Passer's path might still adjust.

It did not.

The Passer arrived exactly when projected.

People moved anyway—but late, unevenly, painfully.

The cost was not higher casualties.

It was resentment.

The idea that some places were granted more future than others took hold.

Online discourse hardened.

Time hoarders.

Interval elites.

General Redding read the reports with growing concern.

This was no longer about safety.

It was about legitimacy.

He issued a private memo that never left his office.

The danger is not that the interval ends.

It's that people decide it was never shared.

Outside official channels, informal systems flourished.

Communities traded relocation windows. Skilled labor moved ahead of families to prepare ground. Entire neighborhoods relocated together, refusing to fragment.

None of it was authorized.

Much of it worked.

The Passers continued their slow traversal, unresponsive to appeals or anger.

Behind them, the earth renewed itself without regard for fairness.

Ahead of them, humanity learned the hardest lesson yet:

Time does not feel neutral when survival depends on how it is given.

CHAPTER TWENTY-SIX

WITHDRAW

Month 15

The first thing people stopped asking was permission.

It didn't happen everywhere at once. It didn't announce itself. It emerged in pockets—small, practical decisions that made sense locally and ignored the larger framework entirely.

A town in southern France dismantled its own relocation schedule and rebuilt it around family units instead of addresses. Grandparents moved first. Children stayed in school until the last possible week. Businesses relocated as clusters, refusing to scatter.

No one filed paperwork.

They just did it.

In the Pacific Northwest, a network of engineers and tradespeople formed an informal cooperative—mobile crews that moved ahead of Passer paths to prep temporary infrastructure, then dissolved and reassembled farther along. Their designs favored disassembly over durability.

"If it can't move," one of them said in a recorded interview, "it doesn't belong here."

The phrase spread.

General Redding learned about these efforts through back channels—field reports that didn't quite know how to categorize what they were seeing.

"They're not resisting," an aide said. "They're reorganizing."

Redding nodded.

"That's the difference between chaos and adaptation," he said. "And we don't get to control which one wins."

Attempts to suppress the networks failed quickly. Not because enforcement was weak, but because there was nothing to arrest. No leaders. No headquarters. Just people sharing tools, calendars, and trust.

Elise Halvorsen watched the pattern emerge with cautious hope.

"They're rediscovering something old," she said to a colleague. "Migration as a skill, not a crisis."

Ancient overlays began to make sense in new ways—not as warnings, but as instructions encoded in behavior rather than text.

Move together.

Leave lightly.

Return when the ground allows.

Caleb Marsh's gatherings changed again.

They became shorter. More practical. People brought maps instead of questions. They traded information—who needed trucks, who had space, who knew how to rebuild water systems quickly.

Caleb spoke only once per meeting now.

"Don't let this make you smaller," he said. "Let it make you portable."

In some places, governments quietly stepped back.

They reclassified cooperative corridors as self-managed zones, offering logistical support without command. It was framed as delegation.

It was relief.

Not all regions followed.

In areas where authority clung to control, movement slowed. Bottlenecks formed. People waited for permission that never arrived.

Those places suffered more.

The difference became impossible to ignore.

Journalists began referring to it as rebinding—the social equivalent of scar tissue forming not where damage was cleanest, but where it had been allowed to close naturally.

The Passers continued.

They neither rewarded cooperation nor punished rigidity.

They passed.

But the world behind them began to look different—not greener alone, but more fluid.

Less attached.

More aware of what could be carried.

For the first time since the disks emerged, the future stopped feeling like something that had been taken.

It felt—tentatively—like something that could be rearranged.

CHAPTER TWENTY-SEVEN

STABILIZATION

The first death caused by the corridor was not caused by the Passer.

That distinction mattered to the people who understood systems.

It occurred seventy miles from the nearest edge, in a hospital that still stood on a map that still made sense. The patient was a middle-aged man admitted for what should have been a routine cardiac event. He was stable. Alert. Joking with the nurse about the food. The monitors were clean. The plan was conservative intervention and discharge within forty-eight hours.

At 03:17 a.m., his heart stopped.

There was no equipment failure. No misstep. No shortage of care. The resuscitation attempt followed protocol exactly. Compressions. Epinephrine. Defibrillation. Again. Again.

Nothing returned.

The attending physician wrote idiopathic arrest on the chart and stared at the word longer than she should have. She had used it before. Everyone had. It was the medical equivalent of a shrug.

But this time, something about it felt dishonest.

Three hours later, a similar death occurred in a different city. Then another. Not clustered. Not patterned in a way that triggered alerts. Just scattered enough to feel coincidental if you wanted them to.

By morning, Elise Halvorsen was awake.

She had not been sleeping well since the signal synchronization. Her dreams had thinned, losing narrative and leaving behind only sensation—pressure, alignment, the feeling of being part of a mechanism that did not ask whether she agreed to participate.

She was reviewing overnight logs when the first anomaly appeared.

Not in the Passer data.

In the margins.

Mortality reports. Minor fluctuations. Single-digit deviations no epidemiologist would flag on a normal day. But Elise had spent too long staring at systems that adjusted without announcing themselves.

She pulled the dataset forward.

Then another.

Then another.

Her stomach tightened.

The deaths were not violent. Not dramatic. They were sudden failures in bodies that, statistically, should have held a little longer. Hearts that stopped. Lungs that forgot rhythm. Neurons that misfired once and never recovered.

No trauma.

No warning.

No struggle.

"Show me age distribution," Elise murmured.

The curve resolved.

Not elderly.

Not children.

Middle band.

People whose bodies were already compensating.

Already working harder than baseline.

Already slightly misaligned.

Elise leaned back in her chair, hands flat against the desk, grounding herself in the physicality of the room—the hum of the building, the faint vibration of ventilation ducts, the remembered smell of disinfectant layered over recycled air.

And beneath that memory, something else surfaced.

The reports from corridor sites. The repeated, offhand notes. People saying the air felt cleaner. That it reminded them of rain that never quite came. Of breath that didn't have to work as hard to be breath.

Elise felt cold.

She opened a secure channel.

"Redding," she said as soon as the line connected.

"I see it," General Marcus Redding replied. He sounded tired in a way that had nothing to do with sleep. "Tell me I'm wrong."

"You're not," Elise said. "But it's not an attack."

There was a pause.

"I didn't say it was," Redding said.

"They're not being killed," Elise continued. "They're being… outpaced."

"That's a hell of a word choice," Redding said.

Elise closed her eyes.

"The Passers didn't introduce a toxin," she said. "They didn't trigger an immune response. They didn't interfere with physiology directly."

"So what changed?" Redding asked.

"The baseline," Elise said.

Silence pressed into the space between them.

"You're saying the world moved," Redding said slowly, "and some people didn't move with it."

"Yes."

He exhaled.

"Say it in a way I can brief," he said.

Elise opened her eyes.

"The environment behind the Passers is cleaner," she said. "More stable. Lower particulate load. Better oxygenation. Fewer stressors at the cellular level."

"And?" Redding said.

"And bodies that were surviving by constant compensation—cardiovascular strain, respiratory adaptation, neurological overwork—lost the context that made those compensations functional."

She swallowed.

"They didn't fail because things got worse," Elise said. "They failed because things got better too quickly."

Redding said nothing.

"It's not extinction," Elise added. "It's selection without malice."

"That won't help anyone," Redding said.

"I know," Elise replied.

By afternoon, the numbers had risen enough to be undeniable.

Still small.

Still deniable.

Still easy to explain away with language if language was your job.

But something else began to happen alongside the deaths.

Admissions dropped.

ER visits declined.

Chronic flare-ups stabilized.

Asthma cases near corridors decreased measurably within days. Autoimmune markers softened. Recovery times shortened.

Hospitals near the altered zones grew quieter.

The contrast was impossible to miss.

In a clinic outside Providence, a nurse noticed she hadn't used her rescue inhaler in three days and laughed at herself for even thinking about it. In Denver, a man with persistent arrhythmia realized his chest felt—unnervingly—still.

And in Washington, in rooms where no one raised their voice anymore, people began to understand the shape of the problem they were not allowed to name.

This was not destruction.

This was inheritance.

The Passers were not erasing humanity.

They were deciding what could keep up.

Redding stood alone in the command room long after the briefings ended, watching a map that no longer represented threat vectors or engagement zones. It showed gradients now—health, stability, adaptation.

He had spent his career preparing for enemies.

He had never trained for improvement.

At a Stayer site near the corridor, Lena Ortiz listened as a man told her his migraines had stopped.

"I don't know why," he said, embarrassed. "I just realized it this morning."

She nodded, careful not to promise meaning where there might be consequence instead.

Nearby, someone else was crying.

Not in pain.

In relief.

The Passer continued its slow advance somewhere beyond sight, indifferent to the stories accumulating in its wake.

And across the world, without announcement or ceremony, humanity crossed a line it would not be able to step back over.

Not because something had been taken.

But because something had begun to be left behind.

CHAPTER TWENTY-EIGHT

REFUSAL

The first official denial was careful.

It did not dispute the deaths. That would have been foolish. Numbers had a way of surviving language. Instead, the statement emphasized uncertainty, correlation, and ongoing review. It reminded the public that complex systems produced noise, that stress manifested in unpredictable ways, that coincidence often masqueraded as pattern when people were frightened.

It was a good denial.

It lasted six hours.

The second denial was louder.

It came from a coalition of medical associations, released as a joint briefing meant to reassure clinicians that nothing about standard practice had changed. The phrase no causal mechanism has been identified appeared three times in the first paragraph, as if repetition might substitute for confidence.

Privately, doctors forwarded the memo to one another with no commentary at all.

By evening, Elise Halvorsen had stopped counting the messages.

They came from pulmonologists, cardiologists, neurologists—people who did not traffic in conspiracy or metaphysics. People who trusted controlled studies and hated anecdotes.

Each message said some version of the same thing.

Something is different.

Not miracles. Not cures.

Margins.

Patients stabilizing faster than expected. Symptoms softening without explanation. Medication dosages feeling suddenly excessive, like clothing cut for a body that no longer existed.

And, threaded through it all, the quiet awareness that the people who had died were not random.

They had been fragile.

Not visibly. Not dramatically. Just… already negotiating with their own limits.

Elise stared at the wall between messages, forcing herself not to rush toward interpretation. She had learned the hard way that being first was rarely the same as being right.

But the data would not slow down to accommodate her caution.

She opened a new model—one she had resisted building.

It mapped adaptation debt.

The cost bodies paid to exist inside degraded systems.

Pollution. Noise. Chronic stress. Compensatory biology layered on top of compensatory biology until survival itself became an active process rather than a given.

Behind the Passers, that debt vanished.

Not gradually.

Instantly.

And some bodies, built around that debt, collapsed when it was removed.

Elise closed the model.

She did not need more confirmation.

Across the country, officials met behind closed doors and failed to agree on language.

If they called it harm, they would be asked why improvement looked like violence.

If they called it benefit, they would be asked why people were dying.

If they said nothing, the vacuum would be filled by people who had already decided what it meant.

General Marcus Redding listened as a briefing officer tried to frame the situation as manageable.

"Say the word you're avoiding," Redding said.

The officer hesitated.

"Selection," he said quietly.

Redding nodded once.

"That word ends careers," he said. "Find another."

At a Stayer site outside Cleveland, a man packed his tent without telling anyone.

He had arrived two weeks earlier with his wife, who slept better near the corridor than she had in years. Her hands shook less. Her breathing deepened. She laughed more easily.

That morning, she did not wake up.

There was no struggle. No warning. She looked peaceful

enough that he thought she was pretending, that she would open her eyes once he said her name with the right tone.

She did not.

He did not blame the Passer.

He blamed himself.

He loaded the car, folded the tent, and drove away before anyone could ask him questions he could not answer.

Others stayed.

Some because they felt better.

Some because they felt watched.

Some because leaving now felt like a different kind of risk.

In one corridor-adjacent town, a city council attempted to pass an emergency ordinance banning proximity gatherings. The vote failed when two members abstained and one walked out, saying only, "I don't think we get to decide this yet."

That phrase—get to decide—appeared everywhere by morning.

On screens. In editorials. In sermons and arguments and late-night calls between people who loved each other and suddenly disagreed about the future.

Do we get to decide?

Do we get to refuse?

Do we get to stay as we are?

The Passers did not answer.

They rolled on.

Elise stood alone in her office as dusk settled, watching a corridor feed from thousands of miles away. The altered ground looked calm. Ordinary. Almost kind.

She understood now why this moment frightened her more than the first emergence.

The world had crossed from observation into judgment.

Not by the Passers.

By itself.

And whatever came next would not be shaped by physics or data or ancient infrastructure.

It would be shaped by the one thing the system could not predict.

Human refusal.

CHAPTER TWENTY-NINE

BOUNDARY

Month 15

The first time the corridor was crossed on purpose, it wasn't a Stayer.

It was a contractor.

His name was on the manifest as Kieran Voss, which sounded like someone who had been invented for paperwork. He arrived at dawn with a small team, two unmarked vans, and a laminated packet of maps that looked almost official until you noticed the seal was wrong.

They parked on the ordinary side of the boundary, engines idling, doors still closed—like the vehicles were deciding whether they belonged here.

Lena Ortiz saw them from the intake tent before she heard them. She'd learned the look of incoming trouble the same way she'd learned buses: by repetition, by the slight change in the air that happened when people came not to stay, not to witness, but to move something.

Caleb was already walking toward them.

That worried her more than the vans.

Caleb didn't walk like a preacher when he approached. No stage posture, no performed calm. Just a man keeping his hands visible, shoulders loose, moving at a pace that refused to escalate.

"Morning," Caleb said, stopping well short of the boundary line. "You're early."

Voss smiled with the confidence of someone who believed time could be negotiated. "Traffic was light."

He handed over the packet. The plastic cover was scuffed, the corners bent from handling. Inside were corridor maps marked with tolerances Lena had never seen published. Clean lines. Clean numbers. Too clean.

"What's the job?" Caleb asked.

"Recovery," Voss said. "Asset retrieval. Non-invasive."

Lena stepped closer, close enough to read the header. Boundary-Adjacent Operations. The phrase had only entered circulation a few months earlier. It already carried weight.

"You don't recover things from inside the corridor," she said. "You document them."

Voss nodded, patient. "That's the old guidance."

"And the new guidance?" Caleb asked.

Voss gestured toward the vans. "The new guidance recognizes opportunity."

Behind him, one of the crew opened a door. Inside were tools that looked almost reasonable—cutters, braces, lifting rigs—until you noticed how carefully none of them touched the ground.

"What exactly do you think you're retrieving?" Lena asked.

Voss hesitated just long enough to seem thoughtful.

"Structures that are still standing. Partially engaged properties. Things that haven't been… fully resolved."

Caleb glanced at the boundary.

Up close, it was harder to explain. No glow. No shimmer. Just the sudden end of applicability. Soil on one side, edited soil on the other. Grass that stopped behaving like grass.

"You've crossed it before?" Caleb asked.

"Not personally," Voss said. "But people have. Accidentally. Animals. Drones."

"And?" Lena said.

"And nothing happened," Voss replied. "That's the point."

Silence stretched.

Caleb looked back at Lena. She shook her head once, almost imperceptibly.

"People crossed it accidentally," she said. "They didn't bring intentions with them."

Voss smiled again. "Intentions aren't measurable."

"Neither is permission," Caleb said.

Voss exhaled, the patience thinning. "We're not here to interfere. We're here to test access."

Lena felt the familiar tightening in her chest—the same sensation she'd had when the first fence went up, when the first advisory softened, when habitable stopped meaning safe.

"Access to what?" she asked.

"To what's still usable," Voss said. "To what's been left behind."

Caleb stepped closer to the line, close enough that Lena felt it rather than saw it—the way space changed its expectations.

"Nothing inside the corridor is left behind," he said. "It's finished."

Voss laughed quietly. "That's theology."

Caleb didn't smile. "No. It's observation."

The crew exchanged glances. One of them checked his watch.

Voss made a decision.

He nodded to the nearest van. "We'll demonstrate."

Before either of them could respond, one of the contractors lifted a compact sensor rig and stepped forward.

The crossing itself was unremarkable.

No sound.

No resistance.

No visible change.

The man took three steps into the corridor and stopped.

He looked down at his boots.

"Everything's fine," he said. "Feels normal."

Lena watched the readings spike, then flatten.

The sensor rig hummed, then went quiet.

Behind him, the boundary did not move.

Ahead of him, the ground did not react.

"What do you see?" Voss called.

The contractor turned.

Or tried to.

His body rotated. His feet did not.

The motion stopped cleanly at the waist.

There was no tearing. No blood. No collapse.

The man remained standing—upright, intact—ended precisely where the boundary decided he no longer applied.

For a moment, no one spoke.

Then the contractor looked down again, finally understanding what he was seeing.

"I can't feel my legs," he said calmly, as if reporting a glitch.

He tried to inhale again.

Nothing happened.

His chest did not rise. Not because it was blocked or crushed, but because the signal never completed. The breath began somewhere in him and failed to arrive where it was supposed to go.

His eyes widened—not in panic, but in confusion—as his body attempted a correction that no longer applied. Muscles received no instruction. Blood did not surge or spill; it simply ceased to circulate with purpose.

The monitors screamed once, then fell silent.

There was no convulsion. No collapse.

His upper body remained upright, balanced perfectly over a system that no longer included him. The expression on his face did not change. Whatever awareness had been there ended cleanly, like a circuit opened rather than broken.

By the time anyone understood what they were seeing, there was nothing left to save.

He was not injured.

He was no longer participating.

Lena stepped back.

Caleb didn't move.

The boundary held.

The cut was flawless.

Voss stared, his confidence evaporating into calculation. "This wasn't in the models," he said.

"No," Lena replied. "It was in the data."

The contractor remained standing, finished.

No one crossed the boundary again.

By afternoon, the vans were gone. The manifest was flagged. The maps were confiscated. A new advisory circulated within the hour.

INTENTIONAL CROSSINGS PROHIBITED
ACCESS SUSPENDED PENDING REVIEW

Later, in the log Lena kept for herself, she wrote a single line:

The boundary does not prevent entry.

It prevents continuation.

By evening, the corridor advanced another few meters, indifferent to the lesson it had just taught.

CHAPTER THIRTY

MISREADING

Month 16

The first press release came before the last van's tire tracks cooled.

It was issued by a company no one had heard of and signed by a person whose title sounded invented: Director of Boundary Opportunities. The statement expressed sympathy for "the incident," praised "interagency coordination," and announced a temporary pause on "unauthorized field demonstrations."

Then it pivoted, smoothly, into optimism.

New frameworks were being explored.

New partnerships were forming.

New access models were under review.

Nothing in the release admitted what had happened at the boundary. It didn't need to. Everyone had already seen it. Clips had circulated for days—poorly framed, shaky, always ending the same way: a clean stoppage, a human body still upright, the camera dropping as the person behind it realized that some lessons did not arrive gradually.

Official channels responded by denying the details while confirming the outcome.

The result was a familiar kind of certainty: one that existed precisely because it was unspoken.

By the end of the week, the corridor had a new vocabulary.

It wasn't a wall.

It wasn't a hazard.

It was an interface.

That word appeared first in a white paper, then in a committee meeting, then in a governor's speech delivered with the careful cadence of someone reading the future from a teleprompter.

Interface implied two sides.

It implied access.

It implied that, with the right permissions, the boundary could be navigated the way a system could be navigated—through protocols, standards, and contracts.

The first misuse was not physical.

It was administrative.

A county assessor's office issued a revised property map that redefined parcels abutting the corridor as boundary-adjacent holdings, a designation that did not exist in state law but immediately began to behave like it did. A bank accepted it as collateral. A developer cited it in a prospectus. A private equity fund used it to justify a new vehicle whose pitch was both vague and irresistible:

Exposure to stabilized land.

The corridor's soil—dark, fine, consistently "better" in

ways no one could fully describe—became a commodity before it became a science. It was sold in lab-grade jars to research institutions that already had it and to wealthy consumers who wanted it for reasons they did not need to defend.

It was marketed as restorative.

As clean.

As patient.

A wellness brand released a product called Corridor Clay with a label that showed an abstract line and no claims regulators could easily challenge. The same brand later released a supplement, then a candle, then a meditation app whose central feature was a looping sound file named Stable Silence.

The app did well.

Meanwhile, real money moved quietly.

A consulting firm with government contracts produced a thirty-page memo titled Responsible Adjacency. It argued that the corridor should be treated like a new class of infrastructure—managed, zoned, monetized. It recommended creating authorized approach lanes and calibrated proximity stations staffed by private security under public oversight.

The memo was shared widely, like all good misuses, as if sharing were the same thing as accountability.

In Washington, a bipartisan committee was formed with a name that tried to sound temporary. It held hearings in a room with cameras and flags and people who spoke with the warm patience of those who believed urgency could be legislated away.

Witnesses described the Passers as indifferent.

Then as predictable.

Then, without noticing, as useful.

A senator asked whether corridor soil could help depleted farmland.

An expert said it supported growth immediately.

The senator nodded, already picturing districts.

Another senator asked whether the boundary could be used to "cleanly decommission unsafe structures."

A different expert hesitated before answering—not because the question was unthinkable, but because it was so thinkable it threatened to become policy before anyone named it as such.

Outside the hearings, vendors sold novelty tape printed with the words DO NOT CROSS in cheerful fonts. People bought it and wrapped it around doorways at parties.

The corridor was becoming normal.

Lena Ortiz watched the normalization happen the same way she had watched the Passer: by measuring changes no one admitted were changes.

The week after the contractor incident, her inbox filled with requests from people who had never cared about her work before.

A venture-backed research group wanted "a brief consult" on corridor aerosols.

A land trust wanted her opinion on "stabilized habitat corridors."

A private security firm wanted "risk thresholds" they could translate into pricing.

None of them asked what the corridor was.

They asked what it could do.

She forwarded most of the emails to an archive folder she had named Pressure, then stopped reading them altogether.

Caleb, meanwhile, began receiving invitations.

Panels. Podcasts. Interfaith roundtables.

They wanted him to interpret the boundary incident the way people always wanted interpretation after an unambiguous event: they wanted it to become a story that didn't require action.

He declined the invitations without drama.

When he did speak—briefly, to a local reporter who caught him between tents—he said only this:

"People keep asking what the Passer means. Meaning is what we do after we stop pretending we're in control."

The quote ran for one news cycle. Then it was replaced by a headline about a new pilot program.

AUTHORIZED PROXIMITY TOURISM TO LAUNCH IN TWO STATES

The program was framed as education.

Visitors would be brought in buses to designated observation points. They would be given pamphlets that explained safety protocols and printed a hotline number. They would stand behind tasteful barriers and watch the line advance, slowly, like a demonstration.

The pilot would generate revenue for local communities.

The pilot would create jobs.

The pilot would "reduce unauthorized approach behavior."

The pilot would, according to the spokesperson, "restore a sense of public participation."

Participation was a comforting word. It made everything

sound voluntary.

Behind the scenes, the same buses were being used to transport something else.

Not soil. That had become too visible too quickly.

They moved data instead.

High-resolution boundary scans. Microclimate readings. Before-and-after models of partially engaged structures. The clean planes where buildings ended became training sets. The corridor's behavioral consistency became an asset. A company offered a subscription service that predicted boundary outcomes for "strategic planning."

It branded itself as neutral.

Neutrality, Lena had learned, was the first language of misuse.

By mid-month, the corridor had a market price.

Not officially. Officially it was priceless, immeasurable, unprecedented. But the way people talked about it—what they were willing to trade for access, what they were willing to overlook to get closer—created a value system even without a currency.

A small town council near one of the corridor projections voted to rezone a strip of farmland as Future Stabilization District. The vote passed unanimously. No one wanted to be the person who voted against the future, even if no one could define what the future was.

A church in the same town announced a sermon series titled The Line That Loves Us. The pastor insisted he was not claiming the Passer was divine. He was only acknowledging what people felt when they saw the corridors bloom behind it: relief, clarity, order.

Order was addictive.

A week later, a contractor's association submitted a proposal to the state for regulated crossing trials.

The proposal included diagrams.

Harness systems.

Liability waivers.

It did not mention Kieran Voss.

His name had been removed from the record in a way that did not require a conspiracy—only paperwork. The incident was reclassified as an unauthorized demonstration performed by an unlicensed party. The party could not be located. The party could not be reached for comment.

The corridor moved on.

It did not punish anyone.

It did not react.

It did not announce policy changes or enforcement actions.

It simply maintained its pace.

And because it maintained its pace, people began to treat it like weather: dangerous only if you refused to prepare, profitable if you learned to plan.

On the fifteenth day of the month, a new advisory circulated across agencies.

It was shorter than previous advisories.

It did not warn of entry.

It warned of liability.

Intentional crossings were prohibited. Approaches were to be monitored. Unauthorized operations would be prosecuted.

The advisory did not say why.

It did not have to.

At the bottom, in smaller text, was a new clause that Lena read twice before she believed it:

Authorized boundary-adjacent activity may proceed under approved frameworks.

Approved by whom, the clause did not specify.

The line of authority had drifted, then returned—not as certainty, but as permission.

That was the misuse.

Not the contractor in the morning fog.

Not the van.

Not the laminated maps.

The misuse was the moment the world learned the boundary did not negotiate—and responded by trying to bill it anyway.

That night, Lena stood at the perimeter and watched the Passer advance another meter.

It did not look like progress.

It did not look like retreat.

It looked like a rule being applied.

Behind her, in the observation camp, someone laughed at something on a phone. A new clip was circulating—an influencer standing near a tasteful barrier, smiling into the camera, the edge behind them like a monument.

They said, "It's weirdly calming."

Lena didn't correct them.

Calm, she had learned, was how misuse arrived.

CHAPTER THIRTY-ONE

AUTHORIZATION

Month 17

The official language changed first.

Not publicly—at least not yet. But inside briefings, memos, and internal dashboards, the words softened and sharpened at the same time. Avoidance became containment. Advisory zones became control corridors. Passive processes were reclassified as non-cooperative systems.

The Passers did nothing to prompt this shift.

People did.

The disappearance in New Mexico was not called a death. It was labeled an incident, then an operational failure, then—after a long night of revisions—an unauthorized exposure. Each phrase moved the weight away from the act and onto the actor, until the corridor itself was once again a backdrop rather than a cause.

That framing held for twelve hours.

Then the video leaked.

Unlike the hovering stake footage, this one was not ambiguous. It showed a man stepping forward and not returning. No cutaways. No overlays. No commentary needed.

Platforms tried to throttle it. Too late.

Copies multiplied faster than moderation could respond. Reaction channels froze the frame where the officer's foot crossed the boundary and drew circles around the exact moment he vanished, as if precision could make sense of it.

The discourse snapped.

It takes what it wants.

It enforces its own rules.

It punishes intrusion.

Elise Halvorsen watched the language metastasize in real time and felt something like grief—not for the officer alone, but for the narrowing of possibility.

Once punishment entered the narrative, restraint followed close behind.

She was summoned to a closed session that afternoon.

The room was smaller than the last one. Fewer advisors. No press liaisons. General Marcus Redding sat at the far end of the table, hands folded, eyes already tired of the argument he knew was coming.

"They're pushing for a perimeter mandate," he said without preamble. "National scale."

Elise nodded. "They believe the Passers respond to intent."

"They believe we can manage intent," Redding corrected.

"That's worse," Elise said.

A policy lead leaned forward. "Dr. Halvorsen, with respect, we can't leave mile-wide corridors of unknown behavior open to civilian interpretation. We have a duty—"

"You have a fear," Elise said quietly. "And you're dressing it up as duty."

Silence tightened the room.

"They don't react," she continued. "They don't defend. They don't retaliate. They don't punish. What happened in New Mexico wasn't enforcement—it was misalignment. A human stepped into a system that no longer includes him."

"So you're saying it's his fault," someone snapped.

"I'm saying it's no one's fault," Elise replied. "And that's the part you can't stand."

Redding watched her carefully.

"What happens if we establish hard perimeters?" he asked.

"You teach people the boundary is negotiable," Elise said. "You turn process into opponent. And once you do that, escalation becomes inevitable."

"Escalation is already happening," the policy lead said.

"Yes," Elise agreed. "Because you're late."

The meeting adjourned without resolution.

Outside, the world kept accelerating.

At multiple sites, enforcement presence doubled. Drones appeared overhead—not armed, but persistent. Registration requirements expanded. Access roads narrowed. The language of safety became indistinguishable from the language of compliance.

Most people complied.

That, too, was dangerous.

At the Cleveland corridor, Lena Ortiz watched the perimeter creep closer day by day—not to the Passer, but to the people. The altered ground remained untouched, inviolate, but the human space around it shrank, fenced by procedures rather than wire.

A young man approached her late one evening, voice low.

"They're saying we have to leave by Friday," he said. "All of us."

"Who's saying?" Lena asked.

He gestured vaguely. "Everyone."

Caleb stood nearby, listening.

"They think if they control access, they control outcome," he said.

"And if they don't?" Lena asked.

Caleb looked past the corridor, toward the dark horizon where the Passer moved beyond sight.

"Then they'll try something bigger," he said.

He was right.

The proposal arrived at dawn the next day.

A coordinated intervention. Limited. Controlled. Framed as verification, not attack. Heavy machinery would approach the corridor at a designated site under full observation. The goal was to confirm whether the altered ground possessed depth limits, load tolerances, or variable permeability.

A test.

Elise read the proposal once and felt her hands go cold.

"They're going to push again," she said to Redding over a secure line. "Harder."

Redding exhaled slowly. "They're convinced the New Mexico incident was a fluke."

"It wasn't," Elise said. "It was a warning."

"Warnings only work if people accept them," Redding

replied. "Right now, they think they can out-learn this."

"And if they're wrong?"

Redding was silent for a long moment.

"Then," he said, "we'll find out how much the world can afford to misunderstand."

At the corridor, Lena felt the tension before she heard the engines.

Heavy.

Deliberate.

Approaching.

The Passer continued its slow, exact movement somewhere beyond the perimeter, indifferent to tests and language alike.

And as the machinery drew closer, one truth became unavoidable:

The next mistake would not be small.

And the system—whatever it was—would not pause to explain it.

CHAPTER THIRTY-TWO

REACTION

Month 17

They chose the site for its emptiness.

A decommissioned logistics corridor outside Barstow, California—flat land, minimal population, clean sight lines. The Passer would arrive there in four days. Enough time to prepare. Enough distance from cities that consequences could be framed as contained.

That was the theory.

The machinery arrived in stages: tracked loaders, drilling rigs, sensor towers, modular barricade units designed for flood control and crowd management. Everything about the deployment suggested restraint. No weapons. No explosives. No language of confrontation.

Just testing.

Elise Halvorsen arrived twelve hours before the operation began and was escorted to a raised observation platform that felt too much like a viewing stand.

"You can still stop this," she said to General Marcus Redding as they watched crews move below.

Redding didn't look away. "I can delay it."

"That's not the same thing."

"No," he agreed. "But it's all that's left."

At dawn, the Passer reached the outer markers.

It did not slow.

It did not acknowledge the towers or the equipment or the hundreds of people watching from behind barriers and screens.

It simply rolled forward, upright and vast, its edge touching the desert at a single immaculate line.

The test began when the Passer was still half a mile away.

Sensors activated first—ground-penetrating radar, magnetic flux detectors, atmospheric samplers. The data streams lit up and immediately contradicted one another. Depth readings collapsed into noise. Magnetic fields returned values that refused orientation.

A geophysicist muttered, "That's not possible," into an open mic and was ignored.

The first physical contact came next.

A tracked loader was positioned precisely at the projected boundary and driven forward under remote control. Its blade touched the altered soil gently, like someone testing water temperature with their toes.

Nothing happened.

Encouraged, the operator advanced.

The blade sank.

Not resisted.

Not absorbed.

Just…passed through.

The loader lurched forward as if the ground had forgotten to be there. Its front treads dropped into nothing. The rear lifted sharply, alarms screaming.

The operator cut power instantly.

The machine hung at an angle, half supported by ordinary desert, half suspended over absence.

A murmur rippled through the observers.

"Pull it back," someone ordered.

The recovery cable snapped taut.

The loader did not move.

Not stuck.

Anchored to nothing.

The cable began to strain, metal singing under stress.

Elise felt her chest tighten.

"This isn't resistance," she said quietly. "It's erasure."

Before anyone could respond, the Passer reached the loader.

The contact was almost gentle.

The edge touched metal.

And the loader ceased to exist.

No collapse.

No shrapnel.

No sound beyond the wind.

One moment there was a machine.

The next there was soil—dark, fine, already reorganizing itself.

A stunned silence fell.

Someone laughed once, sharp and disbelieving.

The operation commander swallowed and gave the next order anyway.

"Proceed to Phase Two."

A drilling rig advanced.

This time the bit did not sink.

It shattered.

Fragments scattered backward, peppering shields and helmets. One fragment struck a technician in the neck, drawing blood. Not serious. Not fatal.

But human.

The rig operator hesitated.

The hesitation was logged as deviation.

The order repeated.

The drill descended again.

The moment it crossed the boundary, the bit vanished.

The rig continued to rotate, suddenly unbalanced, torque spiking wildly. The housing twisted, buckled, collapsed inward like a lung emptied too quickly.

The crew scrambled back.

One tripped.

His boot crossed the line.

He did not disappear.

He screamed.

Not in pain—but in terror.

The sole of his boot began to unravel. Threads separated. Material thinned. Structure gave way not through tearing, but through loss of relevance—as if the concept of footwear no longer applied there.

Two hands grabbed him and dragged him back.

The boot came with him.

It fell apart in his hands.

The man collapsed, shaking, clutching a foot that was intact but no longer trusted the ground beneath it.

That should have ended it.

It didn't.

A technician—name later recorded, face already forgotten—stepped forward too far while trying to stabilize a collapsing sensor mast.

The boundary caught him at the shoulder.

There was no cut in the violent sense.

No spray.

No sound.

His arm crossed.

The rest of him did not.

For a fraction of a second, his body attempted to reconcile the mismatch. Muscles tensed. His jaw clenched. His mouth opened to speak.

Nothing emerged.

The signal failed before it reached his lungs.

Blood pressure dropped—not from loss, but from interruption. Circulation did not spill outward; it simply stopped completing its loop.

He sagged against the mast, held upright by a structure that no longer recognized him as whole.

By the time anyone reached him, his eyes were already unfocused—not rolled back, not dramatic. Just unoccupied.

There was no pulse to find.

No breath to support.

He had not been injured.

He had been excluded.

That was when the Passer reached the sensor towers.

They vanished in sequence.

Not toppled.

Not crushed.

Gone.

Each disappearance precise enough to feel intentional and indifferent enough to deny it.

Elise turned to Redding.

"Call it," she said.

Redding was already speaking into his radio.

"Abort," he said. "All units disengage. Now."

The order came too late for the cameras.

The footage was already live.

Millions watched as the machinery failed—not violently, not heroically—but incompatibly.

The Passer rolled on.

Behind it, the desert bloomed.

Green threaded through dark soil within minutes. Moisture returned to air that had not held it in decades. Birds descended, confused and hungry. Insects followed.

Life reclaimed what had been erased.

The observers stood silent.

No cheers.

No panic.

Just the dawning comprehension that the system had not been tested.

It had been demonstrated.

That night, Elise wrote a single line into her private log:

The Passers do not negotiate with tools.

They do not escalate.

They do not fail.

Redding stood alone long after the platform emptied, star-ing at the widening corridor that would never be fenced.

The mistake had been believing this was a question.

It wasn't.

It was an answer.

And it had been given.

CHAPTER THIRTY-THREE

COMPRESSION

Month 17

The footage did not loop well.

That was the first thing the networks noticed. There was no satisfying moment to replay, no climax that resolved into clarity. Machines did not explode. People did not run. The Passer did not react.

Things were simply there.

And then they weren't.

Editors tried adding music. Analysts slowed frames, circled disappearances, pointed at nothing. The absence refused dramatization. It sat on screens like a dead pixel—small, undeniable, impossible to unsee.

By noon, the phrase controlled test had vanished from official language.

By evening, so had test.

Press briefings shifted tone without admitting it. Officials spoke in conditional verbs and deferred responsibility to inter-agency review committees that had not existed the day before. Questions went unanswered not because answers were withheld, but because no one had the vocabulary for them yet.

"This was not an attack," a spokesperson said repeatedly.

The sentence sounded less convincing each time it was spoken.

In living rooms across the country, people watched the desert bloom behind the vanished machinery and felt a confusion that bordered on betrayal. Destruction was supposed to look violent. Erasure was supposed to leave debris.

This left better ground.

That contradiction stuck.

In a suburb outside Phoenix, a woman paused the footage and stared at the moment the loader disappeared.

"They didn't even fight it," she said.

Her husband nodded slowly.

"That's what scares me," he replied.

At the Cleveland corridor, the mood changed overnight.

The perimeter had been tightened again—not dramatically, just enough to feel closer. More signage. More quiet authority. Fewer conversations that drifted into speculation.

Lena Ortiz walked the site before dawn, watching people wake with the careful movements of those who had slept lightly.

A man approached her holding a tablet.

"They're calling it a demonstration now," he said.

"Who is?" Lena asked.

He gestured vaguely at the air.

"Everyone," he said.

Caleb stood near the edge of the altered ground, hands clasped behind his back like he was trying not to touch something sacred.

"They showed the world it can't be forced," he said.

Lena watched the corridor breathe green.

"They showed the world it doesn't need us," she replied.

Caleb nodded.

"That's worse."

In Washington, Elise Halvorsen read through briefing transcripts until the words began to repeat themselves.

Unprecedented.

Non-hostile.

Ongoing assessment.

She closed the folder and opened her private notebook instead.

She drew a simple line.

On one side, she wrote human intent.

On the other, process.

Between them, she left space.

That space was where the world was unraveling.

Her phone buzzed.

A message from General Redding.

They want to classify the corridor as a restricted phenomenon. Full perimeter authority. They think fear will slow people down.

Elise typed back slowly.

Fear accelerates myth. Myth accelerates misuse.

Three dots appeared.

Then vanished.

Then appeared again.

What's the alternative?

Elise stared at the question.

Acceptance, she wanted to write.

Humility.

Time.

None of those survived committee review.

She typed instead:

Education. And the courage to let some things proceed without us.

Across the ocean, other governments drew different conclusions.

Some closed borders near corridors entirely. Others opened them, framing proximity as opportunity. A few attempted secrecy, rerouting Passers away from population centers in maps that pretended absence equaled control.

None of it mattered.

The Passers crossed borders without acknowledging them.

Online, the factions hardened.

Demonstrators posted videos of quiet vigils near the altered ground. Interventionists called for more tests, bigger machines, escalation framed as necessity. A third group—harder to define—simply watched, silent, counting days and distances like monks tracking a calendar that did not belong to them.

In New Mexico, the family of the disappeared officer received a letter that said nothing useful.

No body.

No cause.

No timeline.

Only a folded flag and a statement about service.

The widow held the fabric and felt nothing settle.

Later, she would drive out to the corridor alone and stand

at the edge of soil that looked too clean to hold grief.

That night, as cities dimmed and screens went dark, the afterimage lingered.

Not of machines vanishing.

Of refusal without anger.

Of power that did not escalate.

Of a system that demonstrated its rules once and then continued, unbothered by whether anyone had learned them.

The Passers rolled on.

And the world, finally, understood that the question was no longer what are they doing?

It was:

What are we going to become around them?

CHAPTER THIRTY-FOUR

NORMALIZATION

Month 17

The world did not end.

That realization arrived slowly, almost offensively so. After the demonstration, after the footage, after the language collapsed into itself, morning still came. Traffic still moved where roads remained continuous. Coffee was brewed. Emails were sent. People complained about weather that had not yet learned to be different.

The Passers continued.

And because they did, the rest of the world began, quietly, to rearrange itself.

Insurance markets were the first to make the shift visible. Not dramatic withdrawals or public refusals—just new exclusions buried deep in updated policy language. Corridors were reclassified as zones of indeterminate continuity. Claims within one mile of projected paths were deferred indefinitely.

Banks followed.

Then logistics.

Ports adjusted schedules not based on destruction, but

interruption. Rail networks re-mapped routes months in advance, calculating around paths that moved so slowly they felt almost negotiable—until they weren't.

In boardrooms, the Passers stopped being discussed as events and started being treated as infrastructure.

Unmovable.

Uncontrollable.

To be routed around.

In Cleveland, Lena Ortiz sat with a small group of coordinators in a former school gymnasium, maps spread across folding tables.

"We can keep the site open another month," someone said. "Maybe two."

"And then?" Lena asked.

"And then we'll have to decide if we formalize," the man replied. "Permits. Schedules. Liability coverage."

Lena looked down at the corridor path marked in charcoal.

"That's how it starts," she said. "You name it. You calendar it. You charge for it."

"And if we don't?" another voice asked.

"Someone else will," Lena said.

Outside, a line of people waited quietly—not to cross, not to test, just to stand near the altered ground for a while. No signs. No chants. Just proximity.

Caleb Marsh had stopped speaking publicly.

Not out of fear, but exhaustion.

Every word he offered was being turned into instruction, doctrine, or provocation. He watched that happen once and decided silence might be the only thing that didn't escalate.

He stood at the edge of the corridor most afternoons, hands in his pockets, watching green life thread itself through dark soil that had once been parking lot.

People still approached him.

"What do you think it wants?" they asked.

He answered the same way every time.

"I don't think it wants," he said. "I think it's finished wanting."

Some nodded.

Some left angry.

Some stayed.

Elise Halvorsen's work became harder in a different way.

The science had stabilized. The models now converged within tolerances she trusted. The Passers were consistent. Predictable in motion, if not in meaning.

It was the human variable that refused to settle.

She sat in her office late one night, staring at a world map overlaid with corridor paths, and realized something she hadn't allowed herself to articulate before.

They were not temporary.

No acceleration had been observed.

No deceleration either.

At current speed, some Passers would take centuries to complete their paths.

Others would never finish at all.

This was not a phase.

This was a restructuring of time.

She wrote it down and then crossed it out.

That phrasing would terrify people.

So she rewrote it.

The Passers introduce a new timescale. Human systems must decide whether to synchronize or fracture.

She saved the file and shut down her terminal.

Across the ocean, a small coastal nation announced it would align development plans with corridor forecasts, drawing applause from some quarters and condemnation from others.

In a mountain town in Italy, residents voted to dismantle an entire district in advance of a Passer's arrival, relocating stone by stone to higher ground. They called it preservation.

In a desert community in Nevada, people refused to leave at all.

They called it faith.

None of these choices stopped the Passers.

But all of them changed what came after.

Near the Ohio River, the abandoned trucks from an earlier failure stood half-sunk, rust beginning to claim them. Grass grew around their tires. Birds nested in open cabs.

They were becoming landmarks.

Children would grow up assuming they had always been there.

That night, Lena walked the perimeter alone.

She stopped where the altered ground met ordinary earth and knelt, touching the soil gently with her fingertips. It was cool. Alive. Indifferent.

She understood then that the danger was no longer misunderstanding the Passers.

It was misunderstanding ourselves.

Because adaptation did not announce itself as loss.

It arrived as routine.

As schedules.

As policies.

As quiet acceptance that the world now had edges where it hadn't before—and that life would simply arrange itself around them.

The Passers rolled on.

And behind them, civilization did what it had always done when faced with something it could not stop.

It reorganized.

CHAPTER THIRTY-FIVE

PERSISTENCE

Month 19

The first structures built for the corridors were temporary.

No one trusted permanence yet. Everything was framed as provisional—lightweight shelters, observation decks that could be dismantled, modular walkways set back from the altered ground. The language of restraint remained important. It allowed people to tell themselves they were still choosing.

But the structures kept returning.

In the Pacific Northwest, a timber town erected a raised platform overlooking a corridor bend, citing tourism management and safety. In South America, a coalition of farmers rotated crops in concentric arcs around altered soil, tracking yield differences like omens. In Southeast Asia, monks petitioned to relocate a monastery so its central courtyard would open directly onto a corridor path.

None of it was coordinated.

Which made it stronger.

At a site outside Cleveland, a group arrived before dawn

with materials already sorted. They did not ask permission. They did not bring banners. They moved quietly, efficiently, assembling a low ring of seating just outside the boundary—wooden benches, smooth stones, lantern hooks.

Lena Ortiz found them there when the sun rose.

"This isn't approved," she said, though the word felt thin even as she spoke it.

One of the builders—a woman with dirt under her nails and calm in her posture—met her gaze.

"We're not building on it," the woman said. "We're building with it."

Lena looked at the structure.

It was simple.

Respectful.

Dangerous.

Caleb arrived an hour later and stopped short when he saw it.

"They're aligning," he said.

"Yes," Lena replied. "Without asking what alignment costs."

The gatherings began that evening.

Not sermons. Not rituals. Just presence. People sat facing the corridor in silence as the Passer rolled past miles away, its movement imperceptible without instruments.

As dusk settled, the air changed.

Not dramatically. Not enough to name at first. Just a softening—like the moment after rainfall when dust has settled but the ground is still dry. The smell carried faintly across the benches: clean mineral notes, a hint of green, something reminiscent of stone after weather. People inhaled without realizing they were doing it.

Someone shifted closer to the boundary.

Another leaned back, eyes closed.

No one commented on it.

Someone started calling the practice standing watch.

The name spread.

Online, the movement fractured instantly.

Some called it surrender.

Others called it sanity.

A third group—small but loud—declared it the first honest response humanity had managed.

Caleb was asked to speak.

He refused.

Which made him more important than if he had agreed.

At one gathering, a man stood and began explaining how the Passers represented a corrective intelligence—how the altered ground proved the planet itself was capable of healing if humans stopped interfering.

He was articulate. Convincing.

Caleb listened from the edge.

When it ended, someone turned to him expectantly.

Caleb shook his head.

"Be careful," he said quietly. "You're turning observation into obedience."

The man smiled.

"Or maybe," he said, "you're afraid of being corrected."

That sentence traveled.

It appeared on signs. On feeds. In comment sections beneath footage of blooming corridors and quiet crowds.

Afraid of being corrected.

Governments noticed.

So did investors.

Funding flowed toward corridor-adjacent developments framed as resilient futures. Entire communities began planning relocation not away from the Passers, but toward them.

Elise Halvorsen watched this from a distance and felt a cold familiarity settle in.

"They're mythologizing adaptation," she told General Redding over a secure channel. "Which means someone will try to institutionalize it."

"And when that happens?" Redding asked.

"Someone will decide who deserves to be close," Elise replied.

In one city council meeting broadcast live, a proposal was introduced to prioritize housing near a corridor for residents with chronic illness, citing documented health stabilization.

The room erupted.

Who qualified?

Who decided?

What happened when demand exceeded proximity?

The proposal failed—but only narrowly.

The idea survived.

That night, Lena walked the corridor perimeter as a larger-than-usual crowd gathered. Some held candles. Others held nothing at all.

The altered ground glowed faintly in lantern light, green life threading through soil that no longer belonged to anyone. The air carried that same quiet scent again—clean, calming, faintly reassuring in a way that made Lena uneasy.

A woman approached her, eyes bright.

"It's choosing us," she said.

Lena shook her head.

"No," she said. "We're choosing it."

The woman frowned, unsettled by the distinction.

Behind them, Caleb watched the crowd and understood something he hadn't wanted to name.

This wasn't worship.

Not yet.

It was alignment without accountability.

Which was worse.

The Passer rolled on.

And behind it, humanity took another step—not toward understanding, but toward meaning.

And meaning, once claimed, demanded loyalty.

CHAPTER THIRTY-SIX

DURATION

Month 20

The first list was never called a list.

It appeared as a set of guidelines issued by a private consortium managing a corridor-adjacent development outside Sacramento. The document was framed as logistical—occupancy caps, access schedules, health prioritization protocols. It cited data. It cited outcomes. It cited necessity.

It did not cite ethics.

Eligibility was defined by vulnerability indices and projected benefit curves. People whose conditions showed measurable improvement near the altered ground were ranked higher. People whose health profiles showed instability were flagged for monitoring.

No one used the word denied.

They used deferred.

At first, it looked reasonable.

A woman with severe asthma moved closer to the corridor and reduced her medication by half. A child with a congenital heart defect stabilized. An elderly man slept through the night for the first time in years.

The successes were undeniable.

Which made the omissions quieter.

A family applied together and received a split response. The father was approved. The mother deferred. The child pending further review.

They were told it was temporary.

It never was.

Lena Ortiz read the guidelines twice and felt something in her chest go cold.

"This is selection by optimization," she said.

The coordinator across from her did not argue.

"It's triage," he replied. "We're making the best use of limited proximity."

"Proximity to what?" Lena asked. "A process that never asked to be optimized?"

The man sighed.

"People are already choosing," he said. "We're just formalizing it."

Outside, the watch gatherings had changed tone.

Silence gave way to instruction. People corrected one another's posture, spacing, behavior. Proximity became a currency—measured, allocated, guarded.

Someone began wearing a badge.

Then several people did.

Not identical—no symbol yet—but similar enough to feel intentional.

Caleb watched it happen from the edge and felt the familiar tightening that came before fracture.

He stepped into a gathering one evening and spoke without being invited.

"You're turning closeness into meaning," he said. "That never ends well."

A woman near the front looked at him calmly.

"We're responding to reality," she said. "You're clinging to equality that no longer exists."

Caleb swallowed.

"It never existed," he said. "We just pretended harder."

The crowd murmured.

Not anger.

Calculation.

Elise Halvorsen saw the same patterns from her office, overlaid in heat maps and policy briefs.

Access gradients. Resource clustering. Health stratification.

Selection without biology.

She sent a warning memo that was acknowledged and archived.

General Redding read it alone.

"They're building a hierarchy," he said into his recorder. "And calling it adaptation."

The first act of enforcement happened at dawn.

A group of Stayers attempted to enter a corridor-adjacent settlement without authorization. They had slept nearby for weeks. They had helped build shelters. They believed presence equaled belonging.

They were stopped by volunteers.

Not armed.

Firm.

"You can't stay here," one of them said. "You're not approved."

"Approved by who?" a man asked.

"By the process," the volunteer replied.

The argument lasted twelve minutes.

It ended when one Stayer tried to step closer and was physically blocked.

No one was hurt.

But everyone saw it.

The footage spread slower than the demonstration videos.

That made it worse.

People watched it all the way through.

In Cleveland, Lena stood at the perimeter and watched a woman cry because her sister had been assigned to a different zone.

"They say it's better for us," the woman said. "They say it's safer."

Lena didn't answer.

Because safety was no longer the point.

The Passer rolled on, indifferent to lists and badges and settlements that rose in its wake.

Behind it, the ground bloomed evenly—no preference, no sorting, no denial.

The cruelty was entirely human.

And for the first time since the emergence, Elise allowed herself to write a sentence she had avoided.

This is not adaptation.

This is governance without consent.

The chapter would not be in any report.

But it would shape what came next.

CHAPTER THIRTY-SEVEN

ACCEPTANCE

Month 20

The settlement failed on a Tuesday.

Not dramatically. Not all at once. It failed the way things fail when they've been pretending to work for longer than they should have.

The corridor-adjacent site outside Sacramento had grown quickly—too quickly for trust to keep up. Modular housing stacked outward in careful rings. Walkways threaded between structures. Access points multiplied, each with its own rules, its own volunteers, its own interpretations of approval.

No one could say exactly who was in charge anymore.

Which meant everyone thought they were.

The first fracture appeared in the water schedule.

Two zones had been assigned overlapping draw times from the same purification unit. The conflict went unnoticed for hours because both sides assumed the other had been cleared. By evening, pressure dropped across the system.

Someone rerouted flow manually.

Another person overrode it.

Pumps strained. Alarms sounded and were silenced. A temporary fix held long enough for night to fall.

By morning, it failed.

The outage itself wasn't catastrophic. Bottled reserves existed. Tankers could have been called.

What mattered was who decided not to wait.

A group from the inner ring—those closest to the corridor—arrived at the purification unit just after dawn. They had authorization badges. They had medical need metrics. They had precedent.

They also had urgency.

A man named Peter—no one would remember his last name later—stepped forward and declared the unit restricted until the shortage was resolved.

People argued.

Not shouted. Argued.

Voices rose just enough to signal entitlement.

Someone shoved a crate aside.

Someone else pushed back.

A woman fell.

The fall itself wasn't severe. She scraped her arm, struck her head lightly against the concrete edge of the platform. She was conscious when they helped her up.

She apologized for being in the way.

Ten minutes later, she collapsed.

By the time a medic reached her, she wasn't breathing.

They tried resuscitation. Compressions. Oxygen. The procedures were automatic now, muscle memory shaped by months of preparation.

Nothing worked.

When she was pronounced dead, the purification unit stood silent behind them—intact, unused, irrelevant.

Her name was Marisol Vega.

She had been approved for outer-zone residence but deferred from relocation closer to the corridor. Her condition—mild pulmonary hypertension—did not meet the threshold for priority proximity.

She had come to the unit that morning because her sister lived in the inner ring and had asked for help carrying water.

The death spread through the settlement like a bruise.

Not loud.

Tender.

Everyone knew exactly how it had happened.

No one could say who was responsible.

Volunteers stood frozen, badges suddenly heavy on their chests. Some removed them. Others clutched them tighter.

The inner ring closed ranks instinctively.

The outer ring watched.

By noon, people were leaving.

Not fleeing—choosing.

Families packed what they could and walked away from proximity they had once fought to earn. Others stayed, convinced the failure proved the need for stricter enforcement, clearer hierarchy.

The settlement split without a vote.

Lena Ortiz arrived that afternoon and stood near the edge of the altered ground, watching people dismantle shelters they had built together.

"She shouldn't have died," someone said to her.

"No," Lena replied. "She died because we pretended we were better at this than we are."

Caleb arrived later, too late to stop anything, just in time to see what remained.

"They built a system that punished waiting," he said.

Lena nodded.

"They called it alignment," she said. "But alignment without mercy is just sorting with rules."

News of the death reached Washington by evening.

It was not framed as a failure of governance.

It was framed as an isolated incident.

Elise Halvorsen read the report and closed her eyes.

This was the cost she had been afraid of—not disappearance, not erasure, but harm justified by improvement.

She added one line to her private log:

The Passers did not create scarcity.

We did.

That night, the corridor bloomed behind the settlement as it always had—dark soil, green growth, no preference.

The Passer rolled on, untouched by grief or lesson.

And for the first time, the question no longer lingered at the edge of the story.

It stood fully formed:

If humanity could not coexist with itself around something indifferent—

What chance did it have to coexist with what came next?

CHAPTER THIRTY-EIGHT

INTERVAL

Month 20

The story broke sideways.

It didn't lead with Marisol Vega's name. It led with a headline about infrastructure failure at corridor-adjacent site, paired with a photograph that showed nothing but people standing too close together.

The photo did its job.

Within hours, the settlement's narrative inverted.

What had been framed as alignment became exclusivity. What had been called optimization was recast as privilege. Commentators who had praised proximity weeks earlier now spoke of it with caution, as if the ground itself might over-hear.

The word sorting entered public language.

Not as accusation.

As recognition.

Talk shows debated whether the settlement had simply revealed truths that had always existed—about scarcity, access, health, worth. Others insisted this was a moral failure, not an inevitable one.

"Nothing about the Passers forced this," a guest said during a widely shared segment. "We chose to behave this way."

The clip went viral.

At the Cleveland site, attendance dropped sharply.

The watch gatherings thinned. Lanterns remained unlit. People stood farther back from the boundary, as if proximity itself had acquired a cost no one wanted to calculate yet.

Lena Ortiz noticed the change immediately.

"It's not fear," she said to Caleb. "It's shame."

Caleb nodded.

"Shame makes people unpredictable," he replied.

Across the country, governments moved faster.

Not toward control—away from it.

Corridor-adjacent developments were paused, then quietly defunded. Language softened again, this time toward de-escalation, community consultation, ethical review.

None of it felt sincere.

It felt reactive.

Elise Halvorsen testified remotely before an international panel that no longer pretended consensus was possible.

"You're asking the wrong question," she told them. "You're asking how to manage proximity. You should be asking whether proximity should be managed at all."

A delegate leaned forward.

"You're suggesting we abandon responsibility," he said.

"No," Elise replied. "I'm suggesting you abandon ownership."

Silence followed.

Outside the formal rooms, something else was happening.

People began leaving on their own terms.

Not evacuations.

Not relocations.

Choices.

In Oregon, a community voted to dismantle their corridor site entirely, returning materials to public use and leaving the altered ground untouched. In New Zealand, Māori leaders issued a statement declining both alignment and resistance, framing the Passers as neither guests nor threats.

The statement ended with a line that spread quietly:

We will not build our identity against what does not know us.

Online, a new phrase gained traction.

The Step Back.

It wasn't a movement yet. Just a posture.

An insistence that not every frontier demanded occupation.

Not everyone agreed.

In private forums and encrypted channels, alignment advocates hardened their language, re-framing the settlement failure as mismanagement, not moral error. Some spoke openly about needing stronger leadership, firmer criteria, clearer enforcement.

They believed the lesson had been learned incorrectly.

That belief would matter later.

For now, the visible world slowed.

At the site outside Sacramento, the abandoned settlement was dismantled within a week. The purification unit was donated to a neighboring town. The walkways were removed plank by plank.

Marisol Vega's name appeared briefly on a memorial page.

Then disappeared beneath newer news.

Elise stood alone in her office that night and watched a live feed from the Barstow corridor. The desert behind the Passer shimmered green under moonlight, unchanged by apology or revision.

She understood something then that she hadn't fully accepted before.

The Passers would not teach humanity how to behave.

They would only reveal what humanity chose when it thought it was improving itself.

The question was no longer whether people would align or resist.

It was whether they could learn to step back without calling it defeat.

The Passer rolled on.

And for the first time since its emergence, the world did not rush to follow.

CHAPTER THIRTY-NINE

CONTINUANCE

Month 20

The Passers did not slow when the world stepped back.

That, more than anything, clarified what had been mistaken for relationship.

For weeks after the dismantling of the settlements, commentators speculated that restraint might alter outcome—that reduced proximity, softened rhetoric, or collective humility could register somehow. That the system, whatever it was, might acknowledge the change in human posture.

It did not.

The corridors advanced at the same pace. Their paths remained exact. The ground behind them continued to reorganize itself with patient precision.

No gratitude.

No reprieve.

Just continuance.

Elise Halvorsen stopped attending panels.

Not because the questions had grown hostile, but because they had grown repetitive. Every discussion circled the same false axis—whether humanity had passed or failed some unspoken test.

"There is no test," she said during her last appearance. "There is only exposure."

The clip was shared widely, then forgotten.

In her private work, Elise focused on what no one else wanted to examine yet: duration.

At current velocity, several Passers would remain active beyond any human planning horizon. Not decades. Not lifetimes.

Centuries.

Some paths terminated in oceans. Others looped across continents in arcs too wide to experience as motion without instruments.

This wasn't intervention.

It was recalibration.

And it wasn't finished.

She annotated her models with a phrase she never included in reports:

We are not living through an event.

We are living inside a process.

General Marcus Redding reached the same conclusion from a different direction.

The military had stepped back publicly, shifting resources toward evacuation logistics and infrastructure continuity. Privately, planning documents had changed tone.

No more contingencies for neutralization.

No more escalation trees.

Only coexistence models.

Redding stood alone in the command center one night,

staring at a projection that showed the world thirty years out—fractured transit networks, rerouted economies, entire regions reorganized around absence rather than destruction.

He realized then that history would not remember his decisions as victories or failures.

They would be remembered as delays.

At the Cleveland corridor, Lena Ortiz noticed the change in people before she noticed it in herself.

The crowd was smaller now. Quieter. Those who came no longer arrived seeking meaning or protection. They came the way people visit coastlines—not to possess them, but to be reminded of scale.

Children stood at a distance and asked questions adults didn't rush to answer.

"What's it doing?"

"Where did it come from?"

"Will it ever stop?"

Sometimes Lena answered.

Sometimes she didn't.

Caleb Marsh returned one evening after weeks of absence.

He stood beside her without speaking for a long time.

"It's strange," he said finally. "I thought silence would end me."

"And?" Lena asked.

"It clarified things," he replied. "I don't need to tell people what this means anymore."

"What do you tell them?" she asked.

"That it doesn't," Caleb said. "At least not in the way they want."

They watched the altered ground glow faintly under moonlight—alive, orderly, uninterested.

Elsewhere, the world adapted in quieter ways.

Cities redrew boundaries that acknowledged corridors without centering them. Schools taught children how to read Passer paths the way earlier generations learned floodplains and fault lines. Architects began designing for interruption rather than permanence.

Religion fractured, then softened.

Some faiths folded the Passers into doctrine.

Others let them stand outside it entirely.

Both choices endured.

The first generation born after emergence would not remember a world without corridors. To them, the mile-wide bands of altered ground would feel inevitable, like oceans or mountains—features to be lived around, not argued with.

Elise understood that this, too, was part of the process.

Not judgment.

Not reward.

Accommodation.

She stood one night at the edge of a corridor and felt something she had not expected.

Not fear.

Not wonder.

Relief.

Because for the first time since the emergence, humanity was no longer trying to win.

The Passer rolled on, upright and silent, its edge touching the world with a precision that never wavered.

It did not look back.

It did not wait.

It did not care whether anyone followed.

And that, finally, was the lesson humanity had begun—too late, perhaps, but not fatally—to understand.

Not everything that reshapes the world arrives to be answered.

Some things arrive to continue.

CHAPTER FORTY

COMPLETION

Month 21

No one agreed at first that it had stopped.

They argued about it the way people argued about eclipses—about whether you were seeing a shadow or losing light. The Passer's motion had always been too slow to trust with the naked eye. You could watch it for an hour and swear nothing had changed. You could look away for three minutes and find the edge had advanced a yard.

By Month Seven, the data suggested a gradual deceleration. Nothing dramatic. No violation of expectation. Just a curve that had begun to flatten.

When the Halifax Passer reached the headland at dusk and simply… held, the first reports came in as uncertainty.

Maybe it's slipping.

Maybe the angle changed.

Maybe the coastline's shifting.

Maybe we're finally seeing it correctly.

It took seven minutes for the instruments to agree.

It took longer for the human mind to accept it.

The observation site had been built like everything else in the last two years: provisional, modular, legally ambiguous. A line of temporary structures on a bluff, generators exposed to weather they were never meant to survive. No permanent foundations. No flag. No sign. Just access controls and people moving quietly in air that now felt—almost everywhere—less hostile to breath.

A mile offshore, boats waited at a distance that had become habit. Searchlights skimmed the water and found nothing to anchor themselves to. The sea was calm. The sky pale.

The Passer stood upright against the horizon like a black refusal.

As the minutes stretched, the air shifted.

Not sharply. Not enough to alarm anyone. Just a subtle change that passed through the gathered observers without comment. The smell was faint but unmistakable—clean mineral notes, like stone after rain, like soil exposed for the first time. It carried from the corridor behind the Passer and lingered briefly before dispersing on the wind.

People inhaled without realizing they were doing it.
No one spoke.

Elise Halvorsen arrived by helicopter.
It settled onto the bluff with unnecessary force, rotors scattering dust and loose gravel across a site that had not been designed for arrivals like this. No one saluted. No one spoke. The aircraft lifted away almost immediately, as if proximity itself carried risk.

She stepped out already knowing why she'd been brought.

Everyone here did.

General Marcus Redding met her at the edge of the cleared pad.

"It stopped," he said.

Elise looked past him—to the bluff, the corridor, the black face of the Passer holding against the horizon.

"How long?" she asked.

"Long enough that the instruments stopped arguing with each other."

She nodded once.

"I didn't request transport," she said—not as accusation, just confirmation.

Redding didn't deny it.

"You were the only person I trust not to ask what this *means* before telling me what it *is*," he said.

Elise exhaled slowly, the kind of breath that came when responsibility arrived before permission.

"Then let's not pretend this is still procedural," she said.

They walked out together into the open air.

From this angle the Passer still resisted scale. Its surface absorbed the last light without reflection. It didn't look like metal or stone or composite. It looked like a decision rendered in matte black.

The corridor behind it—dark soil, restrained growth— ran inland like a seam stitched through what had once been continuous.

"Has it done anything?" Elise asked.

"Nothing," Redding said. "No tremor. No sound. No change in the corridor. It just stopped."

Elise watched—not the disk itself, but the space around it. The minute behaviors at the edge of perception. The way fog refused to gather near its face. The way the wind bent slightly, as if around a coastline that had appeared where none should exist.

"It's not deciding," Elise said quietly. "It's completing."

Redding didn't ask what she meant. He had exhausted that impulse months ago.

They waited.

Time behaved differently near the Passers—or perhaps time was unchanged and humans had simply been forced to notice it. A minute passed. Two. Someone behind them whispered a number into a radio and received another number that meant nothing without the rest of the system.

Then, in the softest possible way, the Passer changed.

At first Elise thought it was dusk playing tricks: a line where none had been—a seam so fine it might have been an eyelash against the sky. It traced a curve across the Passer's face and held. Not jagged like a cut. Not straight like a door. Clean. Inevitable.

The seam widened without splitting.

Space unfolded.

There was no hinge. No opening in the human sense. A portion of the surface simply recessed—away, not inward—as if one dimension had stepped aside to make room for another.

Inside was not machinery.

Inside was structure.

A lattice of interlocking arcs and planes suspended without support, repeating at multiple scales. Large forms nested in smaller ones, each echoing the other with indifferent precision. It wasn't decorative. It wasn't beautiful.

It was competent.

And then the lights appeared.

Not blinking. Not scanning. Not signaling.

Igniting.

Thousands at first. Then tens of thousands, distributed across the interior lattice like a sky turning on. Some were steady and bright. Others dim. Some were absent entirely—dark gaps that looked deliberate, as if something had been removed.

Elise felt her breath catch.

Redding spoke beside her, voice low.

"What am I looking at?"

She didn't answer immediately. She hated how quickly language tried to domesticate the unknown. The moment she named it, people would claim it, monetize it, kneel to it, reject it, demand it choose a side.

She leaned against the railing and watched the interior stabilize into relationship.

It wasn't random.

Clusters held. Proximities suggested network, not ornament. The dark gaps weren't empty; they were missing—tracked absences, like a system that measured loss as precisely as presence.

"They aren't stars," Elise said finally.

Redding didn't move.

"Then what are they?"

Elise swallowed.

"They're status," she said. "They're… conditions."

As she spoke, the configuration shifted almost imperceptibly. Not rearranging like a display, but recalculating. A region brightened by a fraction. Another dimmed. One dark gap widened slightly.

Redding's voice tightened—not with fear, but with the reflex of command colliding with irrelevance.

"Is it reacting to us?"

Elise shook her head once.

"No," she said. "It isn't looking at us."

The realization settled into her body like cold water.

Earth was not unique.

Earth was not chosen.

Earth was one point in a system so old that *ancient* was meaningless.

The Passers were not visitors.

They were not judges.

They were infrastructure.

Maintenance.

And elsewhere—beyond human maps and human time—other lights were changing too.

The field held steady for a long, merciless minute, as if allowing whatever could register to register.

Then the lights extinguished—cleanly, in reverse order. Not fading. Not dimming. Simply turning off, as if a cycle had concluded.

The lattice folded back into itself.

The recess became surface.

The seam vanished.

The Passer stood upright and silent, unchanged from the outside, as if nothing had occurred.

For several seconds no one spoke.

Adults held their breath on a windy bluff like children who had been shown something enormous and then told—without words—that it was not meant for them.

Elise felt the urge to run data, to capture, to reduce what she had seen into a model that would survive committee language.

She didn't.

For the first time, restraint felt less like caution and more like discipline.

"It showed us," Redding said softly.

Elise shook her head.

"It didn't show us," she said. "It completed a process."

Below them, the Passer began to move again.

Not faster.

Not slower.

Rolling forward with the same patient inevitability, its mile-wide edge reaching the sea.

The ocean did not resist. Water slid aside without spray or wave. The Passer descended without drama, disappearing beneath the surface as if the boundary between world and mechanism had always been negotiable.

The sea closed behind it.

Only the corridor remained—dark soil, orderly growth, a strip of land that did not belong to the history around it.

Redding looked at Elise.

"What do we do with that?" he asked.

"We don't," she said.

He waited.

"We let it change what it changes," she continued. "And we stop pretending our interpretations are part of the system."

"That won't stop them," he said.

"No," Elise replied. "But it might stop us from making it worse."

They stood a moment longer.

Then Elise turned back toward the temporary building, toward the rooms where language would be demanded and decisions would pretend to matter.

Redding followed.

Neither of them ran.

There was no need.

The Passers moved at a pace that gave humanity all the time in the world to decide what it believed—and almost no time at all to decide what it would become.

On the bluff, in the thinning light, one fact remained unarguable:

The intelligence had never needed to speak.

It had infrastructure.

And Earth—quietly, mercilessly—was inside it.

Far offshore, the waves continued as they always had.

Behind them, the corridor darkened, green threads rising with restrained certainty.

Elise did not look back.

Not because she wasn't afraid.

Because she understood, finally, what the interval was.

Not the moment the disk opened.

Not the years before and after.

The interval was the space the world had been given—between action and consequence—where humanity still had the illusion of choice.

And now that illusion was narrowing.

Slowly.

Patiently.

As if the planet itself were being returned to an older, quieter instruction set.

The End

CHAPTER FORTY-ONE

EPILOGUE

The auditorium was half full by design.

No banners. No slogans. No live audience beyond the press pool and a small number of observers whose presence was more symbolic than necessary. The room felt less like a confrontation than a record being made—something intended to be cited later, stripped of tone and urgency.

Dr. Elise Halvorsen waited until the doors closed.

She did not adjust the microphone.

She did not thank anyone for coming.

"For twenty months," she began, "we have described the Passers in terms of behavior. Speed. Geometry. Environmental effect. What they do and do not respond to."

She rested her hands on the podium, not gripping it, simply anchoring herself.

"That work is still valid. Nothing observed at Halifax contradicts it."

She paused.

"But it is no longer sufficient."

No one spoke.

"The pause we observed was not hesitation," Elise said. "It was not reaction. It was not response to human presence, instrumentation, or interference."

She lifted her eyes.

"It was completion."

A murmur moved through the room, quickly stilled.

"For most of this period, we have treated the Passers as discrete phenomena—objects moving through our world. The accumulated data no longer supports that framing."

She exhaled slowly.

"What we are seeing is not an arrival."

She let the sentence finish itself.

"It is maintenance."

She stepped slightly back from the podium, then forward again—an unconscious movement, as if testing balance.

"The prevailing model now suggests that Earth is part of a distributed system. Planetary in scale. Ancient. Largely automated."

She did not say alien. She did not say extraterrestrial.

"These systems appear to establish and preserve environmental conditions within narrow thresholds long enough for life to emerge and stabilize."

A hand rose in the second row. Elise acknowledged it with a nod, but did not stop.

"This does not mean life is engineered. It means it is permitted."

She let that sit before continuing.

"The evidence strongly suggests that such systems exist

elsewhere. Many elsewheres."

She paused, deliberately.

"Life—complex life—is not rare."

She waited.

A senior science correspondent stood.

"Dr. Halvorsen," he said, "are you stating that the Passers are evidence of intelligence older than Earth?"

Elise nodded once.

"Yes."

She did not soften it.

"Older than Earth's biosphere. Older than its continents. Possibly older than the solar system."

She clasped her hands loosely.

"What matters is not age, but posture. This intelligence does not observe outcomes. It does not intervene once conditions are set. It does not privilege any particular form of life."

She looked directly into the cameras.

"It appears to be indifferent to what grows, so long as growth is possible."

She took a sip of water, then continued without prompting.

"This is where many analogies fail. These are not caretakers. They are not parents. They are not gods."

A slight tightening in her jaw.

"They are infrastructure."

The word landed with weight.

"Distributed. Redundant. Patient."

Another question came, measured.

"If Earth is part of such a system," the reporter asked, "does that imply intention toward us?"

Elise considered before answering.

"No," she said. "It implies tolerance."

She gestured subtly, as if outlining a shape in the air.

"Once environmental stability is achieved, the system moves on. It does not monitor civilizations. It does not course-correct for culture, ethics, or survival."

Her voice lowered slightly.

"Civilizations are not the unit of concern."

She straightened.

"Planets are."

A pause followed—longer this time.

A correspondent from an international outlet rose.

"Dr. Halvorsen," she said, "is Earth unique within this system?"

Elise answered immediately.

"No."

The simplicity of it drew more attention than a long explanation could have.

"There is no evidence that Earth is central, favored, or complete," Elise continued. "Nor is there evidence that what we are seeing is rare."

She hesitated, then added:

"Scarcity is a human assumption."

She let her gaze move across the room.

"The universe does not appear to share it."

Another question, quieter.

"If this system exists," the reporter asked, "what role do humans play in it?"

Elise's expression softened—not with comfort, but with acceptance.

"We don't," she said.

She clarified gently.

"Not as agents. Not as participants. Not as exceptions."

She leaned forward slightly.

"We are inhabitants of a maintained environment. Nothing more. Nothing less."

The room felt smaller now—not claustrophobic, but recalibrated.

A final question came, almost reluctantly.

"What happens next?"

Elise paused for longer than before.

"The Passers will continue," she said. "They will complete paths that extend beyond any human planning horizon. Some will finish within our lifetimes. Others will not."

She folded her hands again.

"There is no final phase. No reveal. No transition to contact."

She looked down briefly, then back up.

"There is only adjustment."

She stepped away from the podium.

"That is all I can responsibly say."

She nodded once, not in dismissal, but in closure.

As she exited, the room remained silent—not stunned, not erupting, simply recalculating.

For the first time since the Passers emerged, the press did not rush to fill the gap.

They understood, dimly, that this was not a story breaking.

It was a scale settling.

And that whatever came next would not be announced.

It would simply continue.

About The Author

Neil Powell writes speculative fiction about systems, risk, and the quiet mechanisms that shape modern life. His work explores how authority becomes invisible, how compliance becomes voluntary, and how rational decisions accumulate into irreversible outcomes. He lives in Bovina, NY.

The Interval is his debut novel.